broken

broken

BOOK ONE OF THE THIS TRILOGY

J.B. McGEE

To Keri Bear!

Happy Reading. I love
you so much ! ♡

[signature]

To Chad, my love.

CHAPTER 1

June 2010, *Present*

Gabby was home for the weekend from college to attend her friend Cade's wedding. Cade had actually been more of her older sister Sam's friend. But the sisters were close and Gabby had always looked up to Cade as if he were an older brother. Cade and Sam had always been best friends. Cade had proposed to his high school sweetheart, Kristin, just a year before. The wedding was the prime event in Charleston that weekend. Cade's family had old wealth and they had secured Charleston's First Baptist Church for the ceremony and arranged for a slew of horse-drawn carriages to transport their guests from the church to the waterfront Harbor and Battery, which would be closed to the public for the reception. Hundreds were expected to attend. Gabby had been looking forward to the wedding, but more than the wedding getting to spend some time with Sam. Sam had moved back to Charleston in May because she was set to start medical school at the Medical College of South Carolina in August. Gabby had treasured the previous year when both she and her sister had both been college students in Columbia, South Carolina. Even though Gabby was at Columbia College, an all-girls liberal arts college, and Sam was at the University of South Carolina, the girls had shared a downtown apartment. Sam had helped Gabby get through a rough year and frankly, Gabby didn't know what she would have done if she had not been close to Sam during those hard times.

"Gabby are you here," Sam yelled as she opened the door to their small beach cottage. Gabby ran from her room to the door in excitement, "Sam! It's so good to see you. I have missed you so much. How have things been around here?"

"Things are good. Everything is coming along. I'm glad you decided to stay here rather than at the hotel for out of town guests. You know this is your home, too. You're not really an out of town guest. It was nice of Cade to offer it for you, though."

"So, do you want to cook here or go out to eat? I'm starving?" Gabby sat on the old, brown suede love seat in the small cozy living room tucking one foot under her and twirling her curls through her fingers. This was one of the rooms Sam had yet to renovate and its furnishings were familiar and comforting to Gabby. Sam came and sat down next to her positioning her back up against the arm rest so she could face Gabby and tucked her legs in, "I thought we could watch one of our chick-flick movies and order in Chinese food. What do you think? I don't really feel like going out tonight. Tomorrow is going to be a long day. So good to be back together here, Gabs."

"Yep, sounds good to me. I'll go grab the phone, you pick the movie." Gabby hopped up and grabbed her cell phone and the menu. She confirmed with Sam, "Your usual, right?" as she dialed the number on the menu. "Yep, you know me well. I do not like change." Sam giggled.

The girls watched their favorite movie, the movie their mother had loved, *Steel Magnolias*, while eating sesame chicken, fried rice, egg rolls and crab ragoon. They both fell asleep before the movie had ended, Sam on the matching love seat and Gabby on the old, brown couch with empty Chinese food boxes holding chop sticks and two empty wine glasses that had held their favorite cheap red wine on the coffee table.

The next morning, Sam rolled off the couch, ran her fingers through her short pixie hair and rubbed her big, brown eyes. She yawned as she stretched and stumbled into the kitchen to start a pot of coffee, showering while she waited for the coffee to brew. She grabbed a light pink linen sundress paired with a pair of white strappy wedge flip flop heels and a mint green cardigan. She quickly put on a little mascara, lip gloss, and brushed her hair into place with a touch of styling gel. Sam grabbed a travel mug for her coffee and then proceeded to jot Gabby a note so she would not be alarmed when she woke to find her gone.

"Gabs, gotta go run some errands and then I need to study this afternoon at the library. The wedding starts at 6 p.m., I figure we need to leave no later than 5 p.m. I'll pick you up at 5 p.m. sharp. BE READY!
    – Love you, Sam xoxo"

Sam grabbed her purse and keys as she poured herself a carafe of coffee to take with her and she quietly shut the door as she left so as not to wake her baby sister.

Gabby woke up and mimicked her sister's behavior. She rolled off the couch, yawned and stretched at the same time, but unlike Sam, Gabby grabbed her longer dark locks and put them in a quick ponytail. She stumbled into the kitchen and began to make a fresh cup of coffee. She glanced down at Sam's note and it made her heart warm. She loved her sister more than anyone on the planet. It always made her smile when she left xoxo's by her name to symbolize hugs and kisses. It was something their mother had always done on the notes she would include in their lunchboxes every day. Looking at the clock, she smiled realizing for the first time in a long time she had been able to sleep past 7 a.m. It was almost noon and she definitely needed her caffeine. She spent the early afternoon studying on the couch sipping her coffee. She was taking summer classes hoping they would help her decide what she wanted to choose as her major. She wasn't sure of what she wanted to do with her life yet, but she knew her true passion was in volunteer work. Unfortunately, that wouldn't pay her bills so she was hoping to find something she liked and could be passionate about to help her afford to be able to do as much as she could for women and child shelters. It was a passion that was near and dear to her heart.

Gabby lost track of time and at 4:30, she realized she still needed to shower and get dressed before 5 p.m., rolling her eyes remembering Sam having said she best be ready. While she was getting ready, all she could think about was how she hoped there would be cute groomsmen. She had no desire to be in a relationship, but she certainly never complained about some eye candy.
What to wear, she thought. She put her finger up on her lips and made a tapping motion as she stood twirling her hair with her other hand into her suitcase. She had packed a couple of different dresses so she could choose depending on her mood and weather. It was no secret, she always packed way more than she ever needed for a trip.

As a child, she had always been ridiculed about her weight, so she chose her favorite black dress, why she had packed anything else baffled her. She giggled at herself and slid it on over her black strapless bra and boyshort underwear. The dress contoured and accentuated all the right places, while also hiding the places she found herself most self-conscious. Living in the south her entire life, she knew there was no time for straightening her hair, and anyway, in the humidity that smothers Charleston it would have been a waste, anyway. The moment she would step outside there would be waves and frizz despite any efforts to tame it, so she applied a small amount of mousse and frizz serum. She let her wavy hair fall on both sides. The chestnut brown waves just barely brushed up against the cleavage the strapless dress showed.

Gabby was not a girly girl and was known for being able to get ready in a mere fifteen minutes, but that didn't include shower time. So she kept her makeup natural and minimum. She had quickly applied some bronzer to hide that she had not been able to be in the sun much due to her summer school and busy schedule. She applied a light coat of mascara to her long eye lashes. Her hazel eyes were full and wide and they were speckled with hints of gold and rimmed in a dark olive. At 5:15 p.m. she was startled by a beeping horn. Yikes, when would Sam learn she would be late to her own funeral! She grabbed her lip gloss and compact and threw them into her black clutch. She looked down at the shoes she had packed and knew she should pick the high heels she would be most comfortable and least likely to fall in and hurried stumbling out the door, arms flailing and her hair being whooshed behind her shoulders as Sam blew the horn and rolled her eyes at her clumsy little sister's usual tardiness. Sam knew that she was always late. That's why she had learned to tell her to be ready fifteen minutes before they actually really needed to leave, but it was her little secret. Sam smiled at the thought of her secret tactic.

It was a typically hot southern June day in Charleston, South Carolina, and hundreds had gathered at the downtown landmark, First Baptist Church, to celebrate Cade and Kristin's wedding. The church was a prime location for a summer wedding with such a convenient location and bathed in rich history. The girls had leisurely strolled by the church many times and admired its architecture and charm, but they had never gone inside. The large, colonial, stark white pillars made the building seem so grand. There were multiple oversized wooden doors and above each were half-moon windows. Gabby had always loved the Colonial period, and while she was a bit of a tom boy, she had always hoped she would be swept off her feet like Cinderella and dreamed of a fairytale ending. But, she knew that her luck wasn't that good and she would usually try to snap herself out of the daydream before she got her hopes up for too long. Gabby knew her life was anything but a fairytale. As the smiling girls entered the church, they took in the simple but elegant beauty of the sanctuary. The gray walls only helped the elegance of the hundreds of ivory and lilac hydrangeas lining the pews. Each pew also had a large candle towering above it. There were luscious tulle and organza bows adorning each pew, as well. At the front and center of the church, there was a tall arch framing the baptismal. The centered ledge in front of it was adorned with a golden cross, curly twigs in tall vases and several arrangements of matching roses, calla lilies, and hydrangeas.

"Welcome ladies, may I have your invitations," asked a tall woman. She had heavy makeup on, large brown eyes, with a platinum blonde bob haircut. She looked to be in her mid-thirties and it was quickly obvious she was the upscale wedding planner. She wore a black headset in her ear, a black blazer with three-quarter-length sleeves over a silk blouse and a black pencil skirt. Gabby glanced down and observed her four-inch heels. She frowned and thought there was no way she would have worn them for a short event, let alone to work hours coordinating such an important evening. Her thoughts were interrupted as she pulled the invitation from her clutch and handed it to the lady. She heard the wedding planner speak authoritatively into her headset, "Sebastian, please give me the seating location for Ms. Gabriella Gerhart and Ms. Samantha Gerhart."

She looked up with a warm and patient smile as she waited. Gabby tried to avoid fidgeting. It was a bad habit she always had and anyone who knew her well knew it meant she was nervous. She was glad she and Sam had been able to ride together. If she had been alone, there would have been a lot more fidgeting, as Gabby became uncomfortably shy when alone in public, and especially at upscale parties and events such as these. The lady placed her arm out gesturing for the sisters and said, "Follow me, the family has requested that you be seated in the reserved family section," and her smile broadened.

Two teenage girls with long blonde hair dressed in black cocktail dresses wearing calla lily corsages were eager to hand them the ribbon embellished program for the ceremony and asked them to quickly sign the guest book. Just as Gabby put the feather pen down, she saw two ushers on the right side of the church—the groom's side—framing the doors waiting to usher them to their seats. Suddenly, she felt all the air leave her body and she gasped as her mouth dried. She took a deep breath and tried to grab her composure. That was the first time she saw him, their eyes met and his piercing blue-eyed gaze was magnetic.

Sam smirked at her sister's reaction. She pushed her forward so she would be given the opportunity to walk briefly down the aisle with him. Gabby wasn't sure if she appreciated the gesture or not, and suddenly felt flushed and her eyes became large and bright. She tried hard to slow her breathing, but to no avail. The closer she got, the more intense the feelings became. *Please don't let me fall, please don't let me fall, please don't let me be a clutz for once in my life,* she prayed struggling to feel her legs that had begun to feel like jello. The thought of falling in front of him would be beyond embarrassing. When she finally reached the usher, he was waiting with his arm ready to receive hers. His smile was breathtaking, his teeth white and straight.

His southern voice was low and had a seductive undertone, "Hello, Ms..." he patiently waited for her to fill in the blank. His smile slightly shifted as she placed her arm in his, his eyes never leaving hers and she wondered if he had also felt the electricity that had traveled through her stomach and then further down making her entire body feel like she was on fire. She was thankful at this moment she had not applied a blush, as she knew she had achieved that look all on her own; she could feel her scarlet face burning from her blush. She hoped that the throbbing sensation washing over her entire body wasn't obvious to him. Remembering he had asked her for her name, Gabby tried to speak, but her voice was nowhere to be found and still holding his gaze after what seemed like an eternity, she was finally able to quietly mutter, "Gabriella Gerhart, call me Gabby." She shyly smiled, breaking their gaze as she hung her head low, knowing her blush was growing as they began their walk.

"Nice to meet you, Gabby. How do you know Cade? I was told you two were to be seated in the family section," he asked her and she quickly replied, "He's an old family friend, he grew up with my older sister Sam." She wondered how he had known through his implication they weren't actually family. Was he somehow related to Cade? If so, how had she never met him before? Maybe Sam knew who he was. She would have to ask her when they were seated. Five pews from the front, their walk was complete and he was holding one arm out gesturing for her to take her seat. Looking back into his eyes, she found it difficult to pry herself away, but for the sake of not gawking, she politely smiled her most charming smile and calmly muttered, "Thank you," as her head shyly bowed contradicting the tone of her voice. With that, she released his other arm and she took her seat. Gabby was moving her hair away from her face trying to cool down when a few seconds later Sam approached and the usher kindly smiled and walked away as she scooted next to Gabby. Sam couldn't resist and leaned into Gabby's ear, "Gabs, did you get his name?" Gabby could feel her face redden again and she got butterflies in her stomach just thinking about him. It took every bit of self-control not to turn and scour the place like she was looking for someone, for him, but she didn't. "Gabs, did you hear me, the guy who walked you in, he was *hot*! Did you get his name? He never took his eyes off you. I don't know how he could even see where he was going." Gabby had forgotten for a moment she was supposed to answer her sister and looked up a little disoriented from her thoughts, "Yes, I mean no, ugh I mean yes he is hot and no I didn't get his name. He seemed to know we weren't family, though. I thought maybe you knew him. I was going to ask you, but clearly you don't know him, either."

She frowned at the thought she might never know his name, how could she have missed that perfect opportunity to ask such a simple question? That's okay, though. She had no intention of doing anything other than looking at him, the eye candy she had earlier hoped for while getting ready. Gabby reassured herself and held her head high releasing a sigh and a smile. "Well, it was obvious there was something between you two, I could even feel the electricity. I just would have thought you would have gotten his name, that's all. I wonder how he knows Cade. I have definitely never met him before, I would remember that face and *O.M.G* those perfect blue eyes." Sam leaned closer to Gabby whispering into her ear.

Gabby sighed, rolled her eyes at herself and shook her head disapprovingly as the string quartet started Pachelbel's Canon in D. Everyone hushed and turned toward the back of the church, still seated. Here was her chance to look without being obvious. She opened her program and thought quickly that perhaps, if she was lucky, the wedding planner had lined the ushers up in the order in which their names appeared in the program. But it became evident quickly that the names were in alphabetical order and the men ordered by height. Why couldn't anything ever be easy for her? She drew a small half smile because the thought had become almost comical. Shaking her head again, she thought, no, easy and Gabby don't go together in the same sentence.

The list of groomsmen started with the name, Bradley Banks. She wondered if he looked like a Bradley. Geez, how ridiculous, she thought. Did she honestly think she could figure out his name based on the way he looked? It sounded strong and sexy. She smiled because she liked it thinking it suited him, recalling the brief moments she had been on his arm. She could tell that he spent a lot of time at the gym. Through his tux she could tell that his arms and shoulders were muscular, much wider than his waist. His suit was just snug enough to show that what was beneath would not be a disappointment. She swallowed as she quickly tried to dismiss her wandering thoughts about what was beneath his tux. She had drank in his features and tried to memorize his face. He had messy black hair that she could imagine would be soft, clean and perfect for fingers to slide through. He was clean-shaven and had a masculine, rigid square jaw. He could have easily been a model for Calvin Klein. His blue eyes were rimmed in a darker navy blue. She couldn't decide if it was that feature or the black, naturally arched eyebrows that were above them that made them so piercing. There was always something she loved about a guy with dark features and blue eyes. But, she resigned that she had never seen eyes as beautiful as his. The man was near perfection.

She made a subtle sound and smiled when she thought again of running her fingers through his hair. Sam nudged her, "Hey, snap out of it over there," she whispered and smiled a wry smile. The sisters had a way of knowing what the other was thinking and Sam knew Gabby had not just made that sound because of the bridesmaids' dresses. Gabby grinned and put her head down trying not to giggle out loud like a giddy teenager, she slid her program down committing to forget about him, well at least for the next twenty minutes or so until the formalities were finished. She was, after all in a church, and she was certainly lusting after some stranger, gorgeous stranger, but a stranger no less.

He was one of the last groomsmen. As soon as he stepped into the aisle, he immediately met her gaze and he smiled a small smile before turning his eyes to others, to familiar faces. He could feel her gaze and tried hard not to make it too obvious she was the only person he could think about. She was beautiful. She wasn't like the other girls he had dated. She wasn't stick thin and she certainly didn't have blonde straight hair. He wondered if she would be as fun as she looked. Quickly, he tried to dismiss his thoughts, but oh how he loved weddings. It was the perfect opportunity to meet chicks without committing to them, because in most cases, he would leave to go home and never have to speak to them again. But, something was different this time. She didn't fit his type at all and the thought of never seeing that gorgeous face, those curves, well, the thought was disarming. What was it about her? Who was she and why was she seated with his family, but yet he'd never heard of her or met her before? He knew he would have to ask Cade about her at the first moment he was available. He reached his mark and turned with a big grin on his face. He couldn't help but quickly look in her direction. What he had felt when he first saw her, what he had felt when she touched him, they were not familiar feelings. What's more is that he found letting her hand go one of the most difficult things he had ever had to do. He would make it his mission for the night to find out who she was and if his prayer was answered, he'd get to wrap his arms around those curves during a slow dance at the reception.

As he settled into his place, Gabby noticed that he was looking at another girl a few rows up from her smiling sweetly. All she could see was her profile and the back of her head. She could tell she was a tall girl and she had perfectly straight black hair. She looked like she should be a model, maybe she was a model. She wondered if that was his sister and dismissed the thought quickly. No, she had to be his gorgeous model girlfriend. Why had she let herself feel those feelings and actually daydream about dancing with him at the reception? There was no way he could actually be single looking like that. Yes, that had to be his girlfriend. She could feel his gaze as she looked up and met his blazing blue eyes alight with fire. How could she just feel his stare like that? It made her stomach flutter again and she found her hands fidgeting in her lap. They looked into each other's eyes for a brief, all too brief moment, and he was gone again. What a jerk, she thought. Who would flirt with another girl, look at another girl like

that with your girlfriend right in front of you? Suddenly, her infatua-
tion turned into anger. She should have known he was a jerk with an
ego. Of course, he knew how beautiful he was. He could have any
girl he wanted, why in the world would he even look twice at her.
Yet, he kept looking at her. How could one man emit so many emotions in such a short period of time? Gabby wondered what her problem was and closed her eyes and tried hard to regain her composure.
With her eyes still closed, she vowed this time not to look at this al-
luring man just five pews ahead of her standing next to the best man.
When she opened her eyes she realized she had nearly missed the
entire ceremony. The saying that Baptist weddings were over in the
blink of an eye, rang true. After Cade placed the ring on Kristin's
finger, the priest announced that Cade could kiss his bride and the
church erupted with applause as he delicately moved her veil back,
caressing her cheek with his palms. He slowly planted a gentle kiss
on her lips for the first time as her husband. Gabby thought it was
the most romantic kiss she'd ever seen, like something out of a movie. A huge smile spread across her face and when she looked at
Sam, she too, was grinning ear to ear at the sight of their friend's
bliss. Gabby momentarily forgot about the usher and giggled with
her sister. Oh, she loved weddings and longed for the day she
would have her own. She longed for the day she would be kissed
like that by a man who wouldn't leave her, a man who would
promise to love her, to make it his mission to worship and cherish
her for the rest of his life. She caught his gaze again and he was
smiling at her and then his eyes left again and traveled to her, and
the thought of him having a girlfriend made the pit in her stomach
invoke a feeling of nausea.

She startled at the organs' commencement of "Trumpet Voluntary."
The wedding party began to file out, their faces bearing huge grins,
arm in arm. She tried to look cool but she felt his presence nearing
and she looked up to see his quick familiar smirk as he passed by her.
His smiles and gestures toward her were as if he had known her as
long as she had known Cade. She rolled her eyes and put her head

down not sure what emotion she was feeling. She felt silly, frustrated, turned on, and hopeful. Did she actually feel happy? The flurry of emotion was something she didn't welcome. Anytime she had ever felt these feelings, they always brought on heartache.

CHAPTER 2

August 2007

"Gabby, are you coming to the back-to-school party tonight," asked Lindsey. Gabby and Lindsey Howard had been best friends for as long as she could remember. Their moms had grown up together and been best friends and the two teenagers were usually inseparable. Lindsey was outgoing and vivacious. She had long, auburn, ringlet-curly hair. Her face looked like a porcelain doll and she had sparkling blue eyes. Lindsey was part of the *in* crowd and often invited Gabby to popular happenings. Gabby, didn't really fit into any one crowd or clique. She was one of the girls who got along with everyone. She came across shy and introverted, but once she got to know you, she was giggly, talkative, and fun, which made her well-liked and well-known because she was genuinely sweet, caring, and smart. In fact, she was nerd-smart, often burying herself in books or romantic movies on the weekends rather than going to parties with immature drunk teenagers. She hated being around drunken people and especially hated the smell of cigarettes. It brought up too many raw emotions from her childhood. Her brutal honesty wasn't always very popular, either. There wasn't a fake bone in her body. Gabby knew that type of girl didn't fit into the scene of the typical parties Lindsey attended.

"Gabby, are you there," Lindsey asked. "Yeah, I'm here. Sorry. No, I think I'll stay home tonight. You know I don't particularly like hanging out at those types of parties. Underage drinking isn't really my thing, Linds."

"Gabby, did you not get the memo? This isn't one of those parties. This party is at John's house and his parents will be there. Should be innocent. It's a pool party, grab your suit and I'll pick you up in thirty minutes. You're not getting out of this party tonight. Got it? Capiche," Lindsey giggled. Gabby rolled her eyes and let a loud laugh. "Yeah, yeah yeah, capiche—whatever Linds. But, if it turns out to be not so innocent and there is any drinking there, I'm out—got that?"

"Yep, loud and clear Gabs. See you in a few."

Gabby undressed and started to put on her hot pink polka-dot bikini. Lindsey had insisted she gets it for this summer. She usually wore tankinis because she wasn't as comfortable with her figure. She had been heavier, but she had lost a lot of weight the year before when she started running with Lindsey. Being a bit of a tom boy, Gabby had only agreed to get this bathing suit because it had boyshorts bottoms and the top was a cute halter top with a bow in the back at the top of the neck. She would never admit to Lindsey, but she loved it and the way it made her feel when she wore it. She pulled on a pair of cutoff jeans over the bottoms and then threw on a V-neck sleeveless white T-shirt. She slid on her zebra print flip-flops and threw sunscreen, her iPod, and sunglasses into her personalized summer straw handbag. She applied her usual makeup, just a little waterproof mascara and lip gloss. There was no need to put anything else on; it would surely be washed away with the water. She ran downstairs and left a note for her aunt, Emma, saying she was going to John's for a back-to-school party and was riding with Lindsey. She grabbed her cell phone and ran out the front door giggling as she saw Lindsey pull up in her red Camaro convertible, top down and her hair pulled back in a loose messy ponytail and oversized sunglasses. Lindsey definitely had a much easier life than Gabby, but Gabby wasn't jealous. She loved Lindsey, like she was a sister.

"Hey, Chica! Is that your new bikini I see under your shirt?" Lindsey smirked making Gabby blush. "Yep. You like?"

"Uh-huh, glad you didn't go with something safe, like you usually do." Lindsey pulled out and turned the radio up and knowing Gabby could no longer escape said, "In fact, I'm really glad you didn't go with the safe black tankini, because I heard Ian is going to be here tonight!"

Lindsey smiled and quickly glanced over at Gabby and it made her laugh to see her friend look so stern. Yes, if Lindsey had told her that her crush of the past four years was going to be there, there was no way she would have worn that hot pink bikini. She would have been far too self-conscious to wear such a flirty bikini.

"Great, just great. You know Linds, if I didn't love you, I might kill you right now." Gabby couldn't stay mad long and started laughing and let herself daydream that she'd get to the party and Ian would just be so excited to see her that he'd sweep her off her feet and madly fall in love with her. That had been her dream for the past four years, and she knew better. Ian was on the soccer team. He wore his sandy-blond hair slightly long and shaggy. She loved his big green eyes. They had several classes together through the years. They were cordial, but she was sure that other than a classmate, Ian had no interest in her. Gabby had not had a lot of boyfriends like Lindsey. She had gone on some dates, but most of the time, the guys had become her best friend and there were no romantic feelings there. She thought back to her first kiss and it had been far more awkward than romantic.

"Gabs, what are you thinking about, over there? You're not mad at me, are you? It's just I knew if I told you, there was no way you would come and I have really missed hanging out with you. I really wanted you to come. I figured since there would be no drinking I had a chance at actually getting you to come and I didn't want to spoil it by telling you Ian would be here. You look great in that suit, don't worry—I'm sure you'll take his breath away," Lindsey said in one almost run-on sentence giggling at the end.

"No, Linds, I'm not mad. I was just thinking that I don't know why I let my feelings for Ian bother me so much. I am not girlfriend material. I should just accept that and just try to be his friend. Being his friend would be better than nothing, right," Gabby shrugged. She got butterflies in her stomach at the very mention of Ian, and she had never felt that way about a boy before. The thought of him rejecting her had been too much though and she was far too shy and giddy to actually make the first move.

"We're here, Gabs. You look great, don't be nervous," Lindsey smiled, closing the top of her convertible. "I'm not. I'm glad you talked me into coming. Maybe this year I should try to come out of my shell some because I miss hanging out with you, too. I promise we'll have a good time." Gabby reached over and hugged Lindsey and then they busted out laughing at their sappy moment. Shaking their heads in unison, they grabbed their bags, and walked up to the front door.

The Martins' house was a large three-story home situated across the street from Folly Beach. Unlike Gabby's small cottage, the home was massive and held perfect views of the ocean. There were white wrap-around balconies on all of the floors. The smaller driveway led to the garage, which was under the house, like most of the homes in the area.

The girls climbed the stairs to the home and before they could knock or ring the doorbell, John answered the door. He immediately hugged Lindsey and then he gave Gabby a warm hug. He pulled away and surveyed Gabby like a big brother and said, "Hey Gabs, it's so good to see you." He surveyed her, "You look amazing, how was your summer?" Blushing at the amazing part of his statement, Gabby held her head slightly down and looking up with her big eyes cordially replied, "Busy, I spent most of it babysitting. It went by way too fast. How was yours, John?"

"Good, went to this soccer camp at Wake Forest with Ian and then spent the rest of the time surfing at the beach."

John and Ian were best friends. They were both on the soccer team and John had dark brown hair, thick dark eyebrows, and big brown eyes. He was not just cute, but he was such a sweet guy. He was always polite and charming. John had formed a very protective bond over Gabby, much like the brother she didn't have. Despite this, Gabby had tried to avoid John for the last year. He was a reminder of heartache for her. Nonetheless, John was always polite, kind, and even gracious to her. He was a true friend in every sense of the word.

"Anyway, where are my manners? Gabby. Lindsey. Come in. Please help yourself to the food in the kitchen. I'm sure my mom would love to see you both, especially you Gabby," John said warmly holding his arm out and backed up to open the entryway.

The girls walked around into the foyer, which had high fifteen-foot ceilings and balconies from the second floor overlooking the area. The kitchen was just around the corner to the right and it held spectacular views of the ocean. There were dark granite countertops, all stainless steel appliances with a chef's range and hood. Located in the center of the kitchen was a spacious eat-in island with five bar stools lined up in a row. The kitchen opened up to the living room, which was decorated in a sophisticated tropical theme décor. Most of the people in the living room were watching television or playing games. Since Gabby kept more to herself, most of them knew Lindsey better than her, but they all knew and loved Gabby. They all greeted the girls, some getting up to embrace them, asking how their summer was spent.

"Gabriella Gerhart! Is that you," John's mom Stella smiled a large smile and immediately opened her arms wide to embrace Gabby. Stella had long, black straight hair. She had an olive complexion, was naturally tanned, and her skin was flawless. She was in her mid-forties, but she carried her age well. It was clear that John got his good looks directly from Stella. It was no secret she ran a mile every morning on the beach, she was tall, toned, and very lean. As Gabby approached Stella, both couldn't help but smile, even though seeing Stella was hard for Gabby because she reminded her of her mother.

When Gabby and her mother, Grace, had joined the same small church as the Martins, Stella and Grace had become best friends almost immediately and loved sewing together. They would hang out by the pool reading the same book, and then they would spend hours talking about their different interpretations. Stella invited Grace over to her weekly Bible studies before Grace was diagnosed with breast cancer and had introduced her to so many people who had been so good to Grace, Gabby and Sam. When Stella had learned Grace was sick, Stella had promised to help Grace's sister, Emma, take care of her. Emma was a young widow with no children of her own. She moved in with Gabby and Grace in Charleston from Augusta, Georgia, when she got the news that Stella had stage-four cancer. Stella and Emma took turns taking Grace to treatments and being her caregiver. They both tried to make sure Gabby's life continued as normal as possible. High school was hard enough without a father, but the thought of Gabby now losing her mother was difficult for those who knew Grace, Sam and Gabby and all they had been through, and all they had overcome.

"Gabby, my dear, you look lovely. I sure have missed seeing you at church. How have you been, sweety?" Stella released their embrace and holding Gabby out at arm's length to look her over to make sure she looked well, she beamed a large smile.

Smiling her shy smile, Gabby replied, "Good, Mrs. Martin. I've been good. I spent the summer babysitting and helping Emma around the house. I went and spent a week with Sam in Columbia. She finished her freshman year at USC and she decided given what we went through with mom that she wanted to be an oncologist. So, she changed her major to pre-med. That obviously has her pretty busy. She took a couple of summer classes to make up for the classes she missed this semester trying to stay on track to graduate in 2010. I miss her so much, but I am so proud of her." Gabby smiled fondly thinking of her big sister. Yes, they had both been graced with intellect, but it made her feel so good to know that good was going to be coming from her mother's cancer. Gabby still had plenty of time to think about college. She hadn't been able to even think about which college she would attend, let alone what she'd study there. Although, she did think she wanted to be close to Sam, again.

Stella interrupted her thoughts and said, "Well, girls, I hope you'll eat up and then enjoy the beautiful day in the pool. We were delighted to have this small party for you all. Are you excited about your junior year?" The girls looked at each other and giggled, oh they were so excited to get to go to the prom, to get their high school rings, and knowing they were almost seniors. It wasn't a rare occasion for the girls to respond in unison and together they let out a big "YES!"

After talking to some of their friends who were playing Wii games in the spacious living room, Gabby and Lindsey went outside to the pool. The first person Gabby saw was Ian. He had changed. He was taller and more muscular than he had been even just three months before that. She blushed immediately as her eyes met his and he started swimming toward the steps. When he came up he grabbed his towel stepping out with a big grin on his face. He walked over and said, "Linds, Gabby, you both look great. Long time no see. I'm so glad you're both here. Give me a hug!" Gabby laughed nervously and hesitantly leaned into an awkward hug after Lindsey warmly embraced him laughing at his soaked self. Gabby knew by hugging him that she was about to soak her only pants and T-shirt. She didn't care, though. She had been waiting, longing, for his touch for the last four years. She giggled as she felt his cold body touch hers and then a sensation she had never felt passed through her body. She wondered if it was just the difference between his coolness and her warmth, but she felt a throbbing and she knew this was something much different. She looked up at his green eyes and she wondered what had suddenly changed and made him so friendly with her. The thought didn't last long. She was so excited she had touched him and hugged him that she could barely contain her delight. She grinned from ear to ear and giggled.

Gabby tried to sound cool and unphased by her reaction, "Hey, Ian. You don't look so bad yourself. I heard you went to a soccer camp with John. How was that for you?"

"Did you hear that, huh," he said smirking. Gabby blushed and shyly replied, "Yeah, John said he went with you when we got here."

"Well, yeah we went there and it was awesome. You know how I love soccer, but getting to go with my best friend. We had a blast. I could have stayed there all summer and been completely content. So, have you gotten your schedule yet, Gabby?"

She had and she was secretly hoping that like last year, she would have at least one class with Ian, "Yes, I got it yesterday as a matter of fact, how about you?"

"Yep, same here. What are your classes?"

Gabby smiled and recited them:

"First Period: Pre-Cal with Shoal. Second Period: English IV with Brown. Third Period: Gym. Fourth Period: Lunch. Fifth Period: US History with Lemons. Sixth Period: Physics with Starks."

She looked up into his eyes. Boy, had he gotten tall over the summer. He was so much taller than she was now. His smoldering looks were melting her insides.

He tried to hide his excitement, he didn't want to seem overly excited that they had three classes together this year, but at the same time, for some reason he was overjoyed at the thought of being able to spend more time with her. Perhaps, this year would be the year they would really get to know each other. Oh, he hoped so. Her eyes glistened in the sunlight highlighting the gold specs in her big hazel eyes and he wondered why he had never noticed how pretty she was before. He had known her for four years and he thought she was one of the nicest girls he had ever known, but they had been casual friends. Sure, they shared a lot of mutual friends, but Gabby didn't like to hang out the way they did so the only opportunities to see her were in class and well, that was class. Besides, he had always had a girlfriend. Ian had broken up with her at the beginning of summer. He had no longer been interested in the relationship. He was more interested in playing soccer and hanging out with John and the other guys. Ian had not thought about girls much at all that summer. But, as Gabby stood in front of him that all changed in what seemed like a moment.

He smiled and with a cute laugh said. "Well, maybe we could be study buddies. We have three classes together this year!"

Gabby tried hard to not let her jaw drop. For once in her life, something seemed to go in her favor. She looked at him in wonder,

"Sure," was all she could mutter.

"Well, as much as I'd like to sit here and talk about classes and studying with you, I am getting hot again. So, Gabby, are you going to stand there with your now half-wet clothes over that cute polka-dot bikini or are you going to join us in the pool for some chicken fighting?" Ian smiled a wry smile. He had never seen Gabby in a bikini and he couldn't wait to see her in this one. The thought of putting her up on his shoulders to chicken fight made him have a moment and he quickly shifted to make sure it wasn't obvious.

Gabby couldn't believe what he had just said. Her mouth gaped open and a flirty smile came over her. She slowly peeled her half-wet white T-shirt over her head and then slowly shimmied out of her shorts. What had gotten into her? She had never acted like this before, but she suddenly felt playful, fun and daring. If he wanted to play, so could she.

Ian's green eyes lit up with an intense burn as he watched her tease him taking her clothes off her curvy body. Gabby was now a good bit shorter than Ian. They had been the same height just three months before, but Ian had hit a growth spurt mid-summer, and he now towered over her. He knew boys in the past had always made fun of her because she was a bit heavier, but this last year he knew she had started running with Lindsey and he couldn't take his eyes off her. She was beautiful. The bikini didn't disappoint, either. The cute boyshorts were not at all what he had expected as her shorts fell to her ankles, he couldn't help but smirk. Trying to hide how much he liked what he saw, he put his finger over his lips assessing her from top to bottom. Yes, the boyshorts fit her personality perfectly, and she wore them well. She was sexy, but still a bit tom-boyish. Her legs were toned and bronzed from running. His thoughts wandered, wondering if she ran on the beach with that bathing suit.

Gabby interrupted his wayward thoughts when she playfully put her hand on her hip and moved her head to one side, "Well, are you going to just stand there or are we going to—" but before she could finish her sentence, Ian grabbed her and threw her over his shoulder and jumped into the pool with her.

Gabby surfaced and gasped for a breath of air before trying to find Ian and smack him. He was laughing hysterically, which in turn made her giggle. She started thrusting her arms forward to forcefully splash him. This prompted Ian to pick her up once again and swiftly toss her toward the deep end of the pool. *Oh, it was on now*, she thought! They continued their splashing fight until finally Ian couldn't take it anymore. They had made their way back to the shallow end of the pool and were both standing about a foot away from each other. He reached his long muscular arms out and suddenly grabbed her close to him in a hug and she thought he was going to toss her again, but this time he looked down into her burning gold eyes and words escaped him. Impulsively, he leaned down and began to kiss her, as if it was only the two of them and no one else existed.

Was she dreaming? She had fantasized about kissing Ian for the last four years, but she never dreamed it would feel so good. She didn't want it to end. She realized she couldn't breathe and then she quickly became aware they were in the Martins' pool at a party with their friends and she suddenly felt shy again. She pulled back quickly panting and looked at him dumbstruck.

Ian was equally as surprised by his actions as Gabby. He quickly wiped his mouth and reading her face he immediately began to apologize, "I'm sorry Gabby. I don't know what got into me. I didn't mean to do that. You don't look happy, please don't slap me. I had no right to just kiss you like that, here, I mean in front of everyone." But this time it was his sentence that was cut off and Gabby quickly put her arms around his neck and their mouths were together again. She gave him a quick taste of her tongue and then pulled away again. Ian's mouth was gaping open, "Wow, what was that, Gabby?" He said it loud and stern enough for her to hear, but not loud enough for everyone else to hear. It was as if they were the only ones around. They both were zoned into each other's faces and their worlds stood still.

Gabby couldn't believe she had done that. She had never been one to call a boy, make a first move, ask a boy out, and she certainly wasn't the girl who would just kiss someone that she wasn't even dating in the middle of a party. Last she heard he had a girlfriend. She began to feel like a fool. "I'm sorry, Ian. I just. I thought, ugh. I thought you had wanted to kiss me and then you acted like I didn't want it. I did, I just wanted to tell you that, but you wouldn't shut up about me not wanting it and I... Well, I wanted more of that, I wanted you to know I liked it. I'm sorry. I should have known better. I know you have a girlfriend. I don't know what got into me. It won't happen again." Gabby quickly put her head down and tried to run away against the water toward the steps feeling her entire body turn red. She felt like she was a volcano about to explode with emotions. She was so confused.

"Gabby, wait," Ian shouted trying to grab her elbow, but his slippery hands slid right off as she continued to move. "Wait. Gabby. I said wait!" Ian caught up to her and turned her around. Out of breath, Ian looked into her eyes, "Gabby! I don't have a girlfriend. We broke up at the beginning of the summer. And, I don't know what this," he made a commotion with his hands and tried to catch his breath again before starting to speak again, "I don't know what this is. The moment I saw you walk outside, I just know I lost control. Come on. Let's go find somewhere we can talk." He grabbed her hand and led her out of the pool. Gabby hung her head low. Gabby was shy, embarrassed, but also secretly smiling a cheesy ear to ear grin at what had just transpired with Ian. She was proud of herself for being so bold, it had felt good. She had never felt this way before. She kept waiting for someone to wake her up, but she knew, for once, this was real.

CHAPTER 3

June, 2010; The Present

"Gabby," Sam said nudging her. Gabby was still lost in thought about the mystery usher when she heard Sam. "Gabby, come on! We gotta get out of here so we can get to the reception. Snap out of it!" Sam knew her sister was lost in a daydream about usher boy, but the real fun was about to begin and she wasn't in the mood to sit in the church any longer than she had to. The last time she had stepped foot in a church was for her mother's funeral and as beautifully decorated as Cade and Kristin had the place, it was a sobering feeling. She was ready to forget feelings for several hours at the reception.

"Yeah, I'm here. Sam, I thought you were ready to leave," Gabby stared at her sister puzzled. "Yep, sorry Gabs. I just hate churches. I was thinking about Mom, I can't wait to get out of here." Gabby closed her eyes as a small tear fell from her eye. She opened them and slightly smiled. She grabbed Sam's hand, "Let's get out of here. I love you, Sam. Mom would be so proud of you." The sisters walked out with their arms around each other's backs and their heads leaning in touching each other. Times like these reminded Gabby of how important Sam was in her life and how thankful and proud she was to have her as her sister.

Gabby thought about what had transpired after her mom's passing as they strolled out of the church and waited for their turn on the carriage that was transporting guests to the reception. Aunt Emma had moved in with Gabby prior to Grace passing away, but when Gabby had left to go to college, Emma had decided to return to Augusta. Grace had taken out a small life insurance policy after she had left their father. She knew when she left him, that if anything ever happened to her, they would need financial help. The money had been placed into two trust funds for the girls to use for living expenses while away at college. Sam had moved back home when she moved back to Charleston for med school and she had interviewed a couple of students to be roommates to help with the cost of the utilities. It was strange being back in Charleston without her mom or Emma. Gabby knew that it was just the two of them now. The thought made her almost cry again, but then she smiled thanking God she had a sister, that she had Sam as they left the church.

The reception was at the Battery Harbor. Money can buy you a lot and unlike Gabby and Sam, Cade's family had plenty of it, old money. They had arranged with the City of Charleston to have the Battery closed for the evening and tents were set up by the waterfront. A live band was playing in the corner at the end of the harbor. The Charleston Harborview Inn, which is located at the entrance of the park, had been hired to do the catering. This is where Gabby had been invited to stay as an out of town guest, but Gabby had decided to stay with Sam for the weekend before going back to Columbia to finish her summer classes. The harbor was beautiful. Gabby and Sam had always loved swinging on the swings in the spring and fall when there was a nice breeze blowing, when it wasn't too hot or too cold. They would sit and talk for hours in between strolling arm in arm around town shopping.

Sam grabbed two glasses of red wine for the girls and she smiled and toasted her sister. "To us, to Cade and Kristin, to being back home together in Charleston!" Gabby couldn't help but grin. She had missed her sister. They went to the side of the deck and were watching the water when they heard the band announce that the wedding party had arrived. They walked over to the crowd to form an aisle to walk through and Gabby's stomach started to flutter again. *Oh.* She had temporarily forgotten that there was a certain groomsman bringing back all kinds of unwanted feelings and emotions. Emotions and feelings she had sworn off after Ian. She took a deep cleansing breath and finished her glass of wine in one gulp. It was time to start putting them back in hopes of forgetting the pain and preventing herself from getting hurt once again.

The lead singer from the band announced each groomsman and bridesmaid as they entered. Gabby was pleasantly surprised when she heard the announcer say his name. Bradley Banks. She had been right. She smiled from ear to ear at the thought of knowing his name. She perched herself up onto her tiptoes to try to be able to get a good look at him. He was smiling a charming smile and he escorted his bridesmaid through the manmade aisle. Again, like before as his proximity got closer, so did the intense feelings she felt burning inside of her body. She tried really hard to not feel them. She wished she had something stronger to drink to dull the uncomfortable and scary emotions he was bringing out in her. As Bradley Banks got closer to Gabby, he looked over, made eye contact, smiled a half smile and winked. Gabby lost her balance and she fell into Sam, which made Sam burst out laughing at her clumsy sister.

"Hey, you can't be tipsy already! You've only had one glass of wine. It's far too early for that," Gabby elbowed Sam at her comment and tried to brush her hair back, trying to regain her composure.

"Sam, did you see him? He winked at me. I mean, I think he has a girlfriend. I saw him looking at this drop-dead gorgeous model girl during the ceremony. He looked at her so sweetly. Why is he winking at me? Smug jerk!" Sam tilted her head to one side, "Maybe it's his sister?"

"Yeah, I thought of that. But, this girl was beautiful and why would *he* be single?"

"This is true, good point. Heck, I don't know. Maybe he will come over and talk to you and you can ask him."

"Oh no, I'm steering clear of him. I don't need a thing from him other than the ability to look at his gorgeous self tonight. I'm far too busy and he looks like he could twist my heart in a hundred different directions before breaking it. I don't have any desire to go through *that* again." She shuddered at the thought of ever feeling that kind of heartbreak ever again.

"Ladies and Gentlemen, for the first time in public, I'm pleased to present to you Mr. and Mrs. Cade Williams." Applause and whistling erupted all around the girls and they found themselves giggling and clapping for their longtime friend. At this moment, they were sure Cade was absolutely the proudest, most smitten guy in Charleston. He and Kristin were adorable and it had been obvious for years that they were soul mates.

The voice over the microphone was back, "May I direct your attention to the dance floor as the couple shares their first dance." The band began to play "The First Time I Saw Your Face" and they started to dance. When their dance was over they were joined by their mother and father respectively for their dances. The next dance was just for the wedding party. About halfway through the dance, their significant others cut into their dances and the number of people on the dance floor doubled. Gabby held her breath as he put his arms around the girl he had been making eye contact with throughout the wedding. She knew it. She knew he had a girlfriend. She just stared at him, defeated, longing for something, for someone, again that she knew she couldn't have. She crossed her arms across her chest and waited for the torture of watching him in the arms of another girl to be over. But, before the dance ended he caught her eyes, smiling his smooth seductive smile. But, his eyes were gone just as quick as they had met hers and he continued to dance around the floor with *her*.

Gabby leaned over to Sam, "See, I told you he had a girlfriend. I'm so over this. I think I'll get another drink, do you want another?"

"That would be great, Gabby. I'm sorry. You'll find a guy who gives you the world soon enough, when you least expect it, they say," Sam said tenderly. "Mhmm, not interested," Gabby muttered shaking her head from side to side as she turned on her heel toward the bar.

As Gabby walked away the song was over and everyone started making their way to the buffet to get their food. But, Gabby didn't have much of an appetite. She walked back to Sam handing her the glass of wine she had gotten for them at the bar. They found a table and decided they would wait for the line to die down before they braved the buffet. As they watched the other guests, he seemed to be in every direction she looked. No matter how hard she tried to make it look like she wasn't looking for him and staring, it didn't work. Every time she saw him, he looked up into her eyes and she would narrow her eyes and quickly look away trying to act like she wasn't interested. She wasn't interested. She was actually quite angry at his flirtatious behavior in the midst of his girlfriend.

After the line died down, the girls prepared their plates and made their way back to their table. Sam went and fetched them another glass of wine. Gabby knew they really needed to eat before they drank any more or they would be drunk far too early in the night. They sat down and as they started, everyone focused their attention on the cutting of the cake. Cade had playfully put his icing-covered finger on Kristin's nose. Laughing could be heard echoing off the walls of the Charleston Market as they had a small food fight with their cake. Cade's dad, Clark, was his best man and he stood to give a toast to the happy couple. The announcer spoke over the microphone once again thanking them for coming and invited them to join the couple back on the dance floor. Sam and Gabby laughed as they watched the other guests dance. While enjoying their late dinner, they talked about their plans for summer, med school, and Gabby's summer semester. When they finished they decided they needed one more drink before they would brave the dance floor. They stood on the side with similar stances casually talking and sipping the excellent red wine, it was definitely not the kind they had shared the night before. This wine was clearly far more expensive. As Gabby listened to Sam ramble on about her renovation plans for their cottage standing, she shifted her weight on her heels and put her head down and swirled her wine. Sam stopped what she was saying and nudged Gabby.

"What," Gabby said as she started to look up. Her mouth dropped and she felt all the color leave her face. A knot quickly formed in her stomach and she felt every sensation in her body tingle. It was *him*. He was standing in front of her, his head slightly tilted to one side. He had both of his hands in his pockets. He had lost his jacket and all that was covering his torso was his crisp, fitted white shirt, bowtie and vest. Gabby quivered as she looked into his amused, amazing blue eyes, barely smiling, he was oh so sexy.

CHAPTER 4

August, 2007

Ian grabbed a towel and Gabby picked up her bag. Ian did not let go of her hand as he walked them to his SUV in the driveway. There were too many people inside and it would be freezing with both of them so wet. He opened the door to his Toyota 4Runner for her. Gabby climbed into the hot gray leather seat, "Youch!" she shouted as her bare legs touched the scorching seat. She quickly put her towel under her and began to fidget with her bag while she waited for Ian to join her. The car was off and it was warm from the August heat, but it felt good. He climbed into the driver's seat and she had thought they were going to talk, but he immediately leaned over and grabbed her face in both of his palms.

"Gabby, you are so beautiful," he said. She felt her face blush and she closed her eyes and smiled. No one other than family had ever told her she was beautiful and even though it felt nice, it was hard for her to believe his words.

"I don't want to talk. I want to kiss you again, would that be okay," Ian asked softly. Gabby shyly smiled and nodded her head in affirmation. He slowly leaned in and as she closed her eyes again they were mouth on mouth. Their tongues danced and explored, gathering intensity and speed with each move. Ian threaded his fingers through her soaked hair and she let out a small moan. Gabby had never been kissed like this. She had never felt these feelings. She had also never kissed someone who wasn't her boyfriend. She knew she was setting herself up to get hurt, but she couldn't stop herself. She tried to rationalize her feelings thinking there was no doubt that after kissing like this, Ian would be her boyfriend when they were done. She felt euphoric at the thought of her dreams coming true.

She squeezed her eyes tighter and grabbed his messy wet hair in her hands and then Ian's lips were gone from hers, softly trailing kisses on her jaw and then around to the side of her head. She could feel his smile as he nibbled her ear, and the feeling caused her to tremble beneath his touch. Her breathing was erratic and she was having a hard time sitting still. Ian started moving back to her jaw then to her mouth once more. She opened her eyes briefly and then kissed him with more passion than before.

The sensations that were going through her were all new, except the butterflies in her stomach, those weren't new, she always had those in his presence. But, the feeling of warmth and throbbing was moving lower. She was slightly afraid of those feelings, but they felt so good. She yearned for him to touch her body, to touch her everywhere. Thoughts of stopping him briefly ran through her mind, but she quickly dismissed them. She secretly reassured herself that she wouldn't let it go too far. After all she was a virgin and had every intention of saving herself for marriage. She had barely kissed a boy. She definitely wasn't going to give everything up with the first guy who came along. Even if he had been the only guy she had ever really wanted.

The heat in the car had quickly changed her wetness from the pool to sweat, but she didn't care. They were both panting and gasping for air from the heat. Ian's mouth moved down this time, planting soft gentle wet kisses down her neck and onto the tops of her breasts peeking out of her hot pink polka-dot bikini top. Ian removed one hand from her hair and gently cupped her breast. His wet locks were tickling her chest sending even more sensations raging through her body. "Gabby," he paused looking up at her to kiss her lips again and her eyes were wide with desire. He smirked and then began to trail kisses down past her breasts to her exposed navel. She threw her head back as her breath hitched. The sensations were almost too much for her to fathom. She felt something to which she was very unfamiliar. She felt like she would bust at any given point. As he went further down her tummy she found herself slowly spreading her legs to give him room and the urge to move her hips slowly took over.

Ian looked up and climbed onto her lap and began to kiss her mouth again, their tongues thrusting to the rhythm her hips had set for them. "Ian," Gabby said unable to stop kissing him. "Uh-huh," he replied continuing to kiss her. "Ian, we gotta stop," Gabby sighed and stopped moving taking a deep breath. She pushed him away.

"I'm sorry, Gabby." He moved and tried to gain his composure. She glanced over to him and suddenly with the heat from the car and their activities, she felt like she was going to suffocate. "Um, if I don't get some air, I think I might pass out." Gabby was embarrassed and lowered her head breaking their gaze and fidgeted with her fingernails. "Yeah, sure." Ian put the spare key from the glove box into the ignition and rolled down the windows. He knew the air conditioning would be too cool.

Gabby blushed and her eyes were large, "So, I've kissed guys before, but I've never really done that before, certainly not with someone who wasn't my boyfriend and certainly not in a car in the driveway of the Martins' house," she rambled never taking her eyes off her fidgeting fingers, she was so embarrassed now that it was all over.

Ian's mouth dropped, so surprised that as beautiful as she was, she had never made out with a guy before. They hadn't even done all that much. She was far more innocent that he had thought she was. He smiled at her knowing he had been a first of sorts for her. "Well, I hope that was fun, and um, memorable for you," he smirked. "Um, yes. Most definitely." She giggled.

"So, Ian, what does this mean for us? I mean, I am not the type of girl that just goes around and makes out with random soccer players at parties. Obviously, I'm not like *that*," she trailed off looking down scared that he was going to reject her after all she had just shown and shared with him.

"Gabby, I didn't mean to lead you on or for you to feel like I would think you were that kind of girl. I'm sorry. We should have probably talked, but I just. I don't know. I just haven't been able to control my feelings since I saw you walking out of the back door. I'm not gonna lie. I want more of that any way I can get it, Gabby. That was incredible. But, I want to get to know you. I was serious about being study buddies. I think we need to get to know each other better before we commit to anything serious. I don't think I am ready for another girlfriend, either. Maybe we could get to know each other and go out some first, nothing serious. Would that be okay with you?" Ian put his hand on her chin and moved her face over and up so her eyes were looking at his. He softly kissed her forehead.

Her eyes lit up, and while there was a tinge of disappointment that she couldn't call him her boyfriend, dating would certainly be a step in that direction and it was certainly more than a friend. She kept waiting for someone to wake her up, but this was no dream.

"Yes, Ian. That would make me very happy." Her smile reached her eyes and he leaned over and kissed her lips one more time.

"Good, now that we got that out of our systems and cleared the, ahem, air, let's get back inside. Hopefully no one has missed us." Gabby giggled at that thought and realized during the time she had been with him she had not even thought about another soul, certainly not thought about being caught in the middle of making out with him. They jumped out of the car and he chased her back to the pool. She threw her towel and bag down as she ran and jumped back in the pool so he couldn't toss her in again. She came up and she busted out laughing when she saw him do the same thing and their splashing fight they had interrupted with their first kiss started again. Lindsey jumped in and yelled suspiciously "Where have you two been?" Gabby blushed and she knew that Lindsey already knew the answer. John jumped in behind Lindsey and he tossed her to the deep end. The friends spent the rest of the afternoon in the pool chicken fighting and enjoying each other's company into the night. For the first time since her mother had passed away, Gabby thought she might be the happiest girl in the world.

CHAPTER 5

June, 2010; The Present

G abby was slightly inhibited by her wine and the ability to speak had left her when she saw Bradley Banks staring at her, as if amused. She felt everything inside of her burning and tingling. Her head felt like it was spinning, and she wasn't sure if it was from him or from her wine. She gulped trying to wet her mouth. Then she threw her glass of wine back, only taking her eyes off him by closing them to try to regain her composure. She had hoped when she opened them he'd be gone, but he wasn't. He was still standing there, and he let out a slight laugh and placed his finger over his lips trying to contain his laughter. Sam nudged her again. She was really enjoying seeing Gabby hot and bothered, having feelings again. She wanted Gabby to find a guy to treat her the way she deserved, but she knew she would never do that if she lived the rest of her life with these stone walls built up around her heart in an effort to be numb. Silently Sam cursed Ian for crushing her baby sister and causing Gabby to lose all hope. Sam nudged her forward. Gabby glared back at her and then looked back up at him.

The music changed to one of her favorite songs, "A Thousand Years" by Christina Perri. *Crap*, she thought. This can't be happening, this of all songs was her favorite song, and she had decided this would be a song she shared with someone special, if she ever found him, if he even existed. He motioned for her in a come-hither motion. His eyes never leaving hers, his smile was becoming more and more amused as he watched her reaction to him. Gabby looked around and pointed to herself and mouthed *"Me?"* He laughed and threw his head back and took a step closer holding his hand out to hers, "Yes, you Gabby. Come dance with me. I've been waiting to dance with you since I first laid eyes on you in the church."

Sam's elation was almost a scream as she pushed Gabby a little more into his arms and the electricity she had been feeling set in her stomach. It was so odd to her because as unnerved as she had been feeling, when she was in his arms she felt her body begin to relax for the first time since she had seen his face in the church. His arms were muscular and strong and he made her feel safe as her posture slightly slumped. Not knowing what else to say to him, she came up with the only thing she could think of, "I love Christina Perri," she said shyly. "Do you now? So, Gabby, tell me why a beautiful girl like yourself is at my cousin's wedding all alone?" Ah, Gabby realized now how he had known Cade. She wondered how neither she nor Sam had ever met him or even heard about him before.

Gabby smiled and looked playfully up into his eyes, "I'm not alone. I'm with my sister, Sam." Gabby glanced in Sam's direction still glaring at her. Sam rolled her eyes and laughed then turned to get another glass of wine.

Rolling his eyes and smirking, "Oh, I see. You're going to play hard to get, huh. You know that's not exactly what I *meant*." He winked as he emphasized meant.

Oh he was smooth, Gabby thought. Part of her wanted to bust out laughing and the other part of her wanted to run far away from him, he exuded trouble. He was going to be bad news and she had known from the moment he had touched her. Guys like him only hurt girls like her.

"If you *meant*, do I have a boyfriend, then the answer would be no," Gabby smarted off to him. "Yes, that is precisely what I *meant*," he grinned wider at the inappropriate thoughts that entered his mind with that admission. "What are you doing?" she asked him becoming angrier with him by the minute. He looked confused, "Dancing?"

"No, I mean what are you doing dancing with *me*? I mean, I saw you dancing with the model earlier. I saw the way you looked at her during the wedding, like you really love her. I mean, she's gorgeous, why in the world would you be looking at anyone else when you have her? By the way, where did she go? I mean, do you what—have an open relationship to where you can just flirt and pick up girls right in front of her? Oh! I know your type. I bet she is completely oblivious to how you charm other girls as soon as she turns her back from you!" Her tone was quick as she vented all of her earlier frustrations with his flirtatious behavior in the presence of this other woman.

"So, I charm you?" He pulled her closer.

"Are you avoiding the question?" she hissed.

He couldn't contain his laughter any longer. She was really getting angry with him. As he threw his head back laughing they both stopped dancing. She dropped her arms, pursed her lips and narrowed her eyes. She turned on her heel to walk away. *No, she was not in the market for being made a fool of on the dance floor.* She didn't know what he thought was so funny, but she would not be laughed at or embarrassed. As soon as she turned, he quit laughing and grabbed her elbow. "Wait, Gabby! Just wait. Let me explain," he sounded exasperated. With his hands on his knees as he panted to catch his breath, Gabby turned and glared down at him with her arms crossed across her chest. He couldn't help but smile again because she had just lifted her cleavage and she looked so sexy he wanted to grab her right then and there and throw her over his shoulder and take her somewhere more private. Angry Gabby was quite cute and he thought he might just have to try to make her angry more often. But, he could tell she was far too mad and wouldn't find him taking her like that very amusing. Gabby sternly raised one eyebrow and began to turn again rolling her eyes when he finally was able to speak again.

"She's not my girlfriend," he panted returning to standing upright.

"Oh really," turning back interested to hear what he would say next.

"No, geez. What's your problem? I'm not here with anyone. Well I'm here with her the same way you're here with Sam! She's my sister for crying out loud. Her name is Carmen. I'll introduce you if you'd like. You said she was gorgeous, don't we look alike at all to you?" He was either a really good liar or he was now completely serious, and clearly he was not oblivious to his unbelievable good looks. *Great, add conceited to the growing list of attributes Bradley Banks possesses,* Gabby thought sarcastically to herself rolling her eyes and then realizing what he had just said.

Oh no, This couldn't be. She had entertained that idea, but the girl was beautiful. But, then again, he was beautiful and now that she stopped and let all the flashbacks enter her head as she took a cleansing breath and closed her eyes, she realized they did look alike. She shook her head as she opened her eyes and then busted out laughing and turned determined to walk away, to get far, far away from him.

"What the hell! Where are you going? Did you want her to be my girlfriend? What's your problem? I thought you'd be happy she was my sister, not turn and run away again laughing. Just stop. Please. Please finish our dance." Bradley wasn't used to running after women, or begging for that matter. It was usually the opposite. But, then again, nothing about Gabriella Gerhart had been normal.

Gabby turned back around and looked at him and her look had changed. She looked broken and sad, "Bradley. Your name *is* Bradley, right," she spoke coldly. He smiled down at her thankful she was finally talking to him, "Yes, that would be me."

"I'm no good for you. Look at you. You're gorgeous. You could have anyone here tonight. Go find someone else. Is that enough talking for you because I'd like a drink?" Gabby turned on her heel to walk away, again.

Part of her wanted to give in to her desires, this connection she felt with him, and run and wrap her arms around him, kissing him passionately as if her life depended on it. But, the other realistic part of her was glad she was walking away. His words echoed in her head *"Did you want her to be my girlfriend?"* Maybe deep down she had hoped Carmen was his girlfriend. As sick as the thought made her, at least then she would be safe from him hurting her. She wouldn't ever know what it was like to be in his arms. She would have just taken his beautiful face home and had him in her dreams, where it was safe. She held her head up high and took a breath. She knew she was doing the right thing by walking away. She had more baggage than baggage claim at the airport and she didn't need to feel these feelings. She was doing just fine the way she was. She had worked hard to build up walls from the emotional pain since Ian had shattered her and she needed to maintain control. She needed to make sure that she never hurt like *that* again.

CHAPTER 6

September 2007

Ian passed a note to Gabby in fifth period. She smiled as she secretly opened it placing it under her history book. She thought back about how the past month since the pool party had been the best month of her life. She was absolutely smitten. She and Ian took every opportunity to make out and could barely keep their hands off each other when they were alone. Ian, however, had decided that until they got to know each other better, they would refrain from public displays of affection. His reasoning had been that if people knew they were affectionate, they would rush their relationship and he wanted to take it at their own pace. Their friends all thought they had just grown to know each other through studying and were getting to being close friends. None of them knew just how close they already were when they were supposed to be studying. Lindsey had an idea that things were more than that, but no matter how much she pried, she couldn't get Gabby to admit to anything more than just studying. Gabby knew this type of behavior was so uncharacteristic for her, but for Ian, she was willing to do whatever she had to do to continue seeing him. She knew he would eventually come around and make the commitment to her she longed to have with him. She glanced down at the note when the teacher turned her back to write on the dry-erase board.

"Gabs. Meet me at my house after school to study. I am struggling with anatomy—Ian."

Gabby blushed because she knew that the only anatomy they would be studying was each other's and now the day couldn't get finished fast enough. She jotted back "Can't wait," and nudged his side for him to grab the note.

The rest of the day buzzed by and all Gabby could think about was being with Ian. Every word her teachers had spoken had been a blur, as if she were an outsider watching the class from above, she definitely had not been an active participant. She was thankful her teachers had not noticed her daydreaming and called her out to answer a question. She quickly rushed to her locker after her last period brushing up against students. Some students yelled at her to slow down and watch where she was going. She grabbed the books she needed for her homework and quickly secured the cold lock back into place. She threw her backpack over her shoulder and with the biggest grin ran outside toward her car. On her way out she heard a familiar voice call her name.

"Gabs, wait up! Where are you running off to in such a hurry," quizzed Lindsey. "Oh, hey Linds. I gotta go. Ian needs to study for a test tomorrow and I promised I'd call out flash cards for him after school." Lindsey laughed, "Okay, I was just wondering if you wanted to go to the party at John's tomorrow night? Do you have plans? I'm sure Ian will be there." Gabby tried not to look disappointed. Why hadn't Ian invited her to John's party? Why was she hearing about it from her best friend? She could understand that he wouldn't want other people to think it was a date, but seems like he could have at least mentioned it and invited her to go with Lindsey. Gabby dismissed the unpleasant thoughts as she was too excited about what she knew was about to happen to dwell on anything unpleasant. She shook her head and quickly blinked to snap out of her thoughts.

"Yeah, I'd love to go. Do you want to drive or do you want me to drive?" Even though Gabby asked, she already knew the answer. It ultimately was a rhetorical question. Lindsey laughed, "I got it, Gabs!" Gabby laughed because she knew that her old, faded black Honda Civic that had been Sam's in high school was not nearly fashionable for Lindsey. She rolled her eyes. "Great, what time should I be ready?"

"Seven okay with you?" asked Lindsey.

"Yep, that works. Well, I better get going, Ian's waiting for me. I'll see you tomorrow. Thanks for inviting me, Lindsey. I miss you. Hopefully we can hang out more now that things are getting settled with back to school." Gabby grabbed her best friend for a quick hug. She was sad that she and Lindsey not only hadn't any classes together, but they had different lunch periods, too. She felt like she hardly got to see Lindsey anymore.

"No problem, Gabby. I told you that I wanted to hang out more, just call me when you have some free time. I've been trying to hang out with John more. We have several classes together. I really like him, Gabs. I wish he'd ask me out, but he doesn't seem that interested. Wouldn't it be cool if you and Ian got together and me and John got together? Geez, Lindsey. I need to snap out of it! Oh well, I better let you go. See you tomorrow, Gabs." Lindsey giggled realizing she had been thinking out loud and rambling to Gabby. "Bye, Linds. See you tomorrow." Gabby smiled and hurried the rest of the way to her car.

Lindsey turned to walk away with her head down and sighed at the thought of John. She wasn't used to not being able to date whomever she desired. John had presented her with a challenge. She thought he was funny, cute, and he treated her respectfully. Then her thoughts went to Gabby. Her best friend seemed so bubbly. Ever since the party they had both professed they were just friends, but they were both acting differently. It was obvious to Lindsey that Gabby wasn't telling her everything. She smiled at the thought of her best friend finally having the guy she had pined for and lusted over for the last four years. Then Lindsey wondered why Ian had not asked her to the party. *Had he even intended to ask her? Surely Ian wouldn't just use Gabby to help him get good grades and hide her out in public and act like he didn't care for her.* She quickly tried to move her thoughts to happier ideas as she opened the door to her red Camaro and slid down the black leather seats.

Gabby pulled up to Ian's massive brick home. Unlike John, his house was farther away from the beach in a prestigious gated neighborhood. It was much larger than John's house. His parents were both doctors and often worked late hours. Ian was the only child and he wanted for nothing.

Gabby grabbed her book bag, although the thought made her laugh because she knew she didn't really need it. She locked her doors, but as she did realized her car was by far the cheapest car in the neighborhood. It's not as if anyone would want to steal it when there were BMWs, Mercedes, and Lexus readily available. The feeling of inadequacy she often felt around her friends rushed over her like a tidal wave. She shook her head and reassured herself that her social standing didn't matter, Ian wanted her and that's why she was here. She walked down his drive and then up the long staircase to his front porch. She pursed her lips to spread her freshly applied lip gloss and pushed her hair behind her shoulders as she rang his doorbell.

Ian opened the door towering over Gabby with a seductive smile. "Hey, you," he drank in her body. "Oh yes, I am having some serious trouble with anatomy. Remind me what this is called?" He leaned in and kissed her softly on her neck. "And this?" He kissed her cheek. Gabby closed her eyes and giggled. "Please come in and I'll show what else I need help with." Ian grabbed her hands and pulled her inside, Gabby giggling with anticipation. As she walked through the door he playfully spanked her supple behind. It completely caught her off guard as she jumped, "Youch!"

CHAPTER 7

June, 2010; The Present

Bradley was now furious. What was so maddening about this woman, who was walking away from him? He was seeing so many emotions in her. First she had been flirty, then shy, then playful, angry, and now she was sad, he shook his head realizing he thought she was sad. He shook his head as he watched her walk back to Sam. No, he didn't need someone so complicated in his life. He had thought she would be fun and flirty when he first saw her and he thought with the way she was reacting to him she would be putty in his hands. He had not quite expected such resistance from her. He loved a challenge, but she seemed very complicated. He had enough complication in his life, he wasn't sure he needed anything else. But, as he watched her toss her hair back and lick her lips before she took a sip of her wine he realized that this woman was irresistible and mysterious. *What had happened to her that made her unable to see how sexy she was to him?* Yes, he knew he could have any woman there, but he had chosen her. She had pushed him away. Bradley Banks didn't get rejected and he wasn't going to start tonight.

He took a deep breath and with narrowed eyes and pursed lips he strode over to Gabriella Gerhart and came up behind her. Sam saw him and her eyes widened. Gabby had not the time to react to her sister's terrified look before Bradley grabbed both of Gabby's arms and forcefully turned her around and pulled her as close to him as he could. She gasped and her eyes widened. Electricity surged through her body and she could barely breathe. She looked up into his fierce blue eyes. They were blazing with desire and in an instant he forced his tongue into her mouth and kissed her passionately. Gabby could barely move. She stood paralyzed by his actions. She was surprised, pleasantly surprised. Oh, she had daydreamed about his lips on hers the entire day and he was so refreshing. She savored his taste as his tongue assaulted her mouth, pulling on her bottom lip gently as he released her.

Gabby tried to catch her breath and seriously thought about slapping him for assuming he could just walk over and do things like that to her, never mind that she had actually liked it. It was rude, in fact as the night went on she was finding him more and more rude. *Who did he think he was?* He had known her for all of five minutes, if that. But, the other part of her now knew that the chemistry they had was not just on her part. She knew that there was something there, something very special.

"Now that you've had your glass of wine you wanted so badly, you will come back and dance with me." Bradley insisted handing her glass to Sam and nodding his head. He grabbed Gabby's hand and they started to make their way back to the dance floor. Sam smiled an unsure smile. *Oh boy*, she thought, *what in the world had Gabby gotten herself into with him.*

He embraced her and started to dance. *Where did he learn that?* Gabby thought. He led her perfectly and she had no choice but to follow. Looking up into his clear eyes she wondered if she would be able to ever resist him. No, maybe not. But, she had to try.

"Mr. Banks, with all due respect, just who the hell do you think you are? Do you think I'm some puppet on a string and you can just order me around? You might be used to controlling other women, but I will not be controlled by anyone. I told you I'm no good for you. Why are you making this so hard?"

"You told me I could have anyone here, and you're right. I could, but I want you. Why are *you* pushing me away?"

"I have more baggage than baggage claim. I'm damaged goods. I'm not good at," she released him for a moment and fingered between the two of them *"this."*

"Well, I think you're dancing just fine, Miss Gerhart," he smirked. He knew that was not what she meant, but he had hoped to lighten their mood. Maybe if he could get her to relax she would give him a chance.

"Ha, that's not what I *meant* at all. You have a way of twisting my words, Mr. Banks. Tell me what it is you do?"

"I own my own architecture company. We design high rises and sky scrapers." He proudly smiled and his eyes never left hers. His head cocked to one side. He liked that she was talking to him. He hoped it would continue. He could watch the way she bit her lower lip as she listened to him talk all day, well probably not. It only made him want her even more. He moved his body a little closer and she was slightly startled as she could feel his length pressed against her.

"So, Miss Gerhart, I know what you do to me, but what do you *do*?"

Gabby gasped at his forward comment and all of the blood in her face suddenly rushed south. No, he could not have this effect on her. She could not be hurt. It was like writing on a billboard that he was clearly just trying to get a good time out of her for the night and she was not in a place where she could do that for him.

Ignoring his comment she sassily replied back, "I am a student."

"Oh really, how old are you Gabby?"

"Don't you know it's not polite to ask a woman her age? Oh wait, you aren't polite. You say tacky things while pushing your erection against a girl you met five minutes ago, brutally kissed, and—"

Bradley interrupted her by putting one finger over her lips and said "Shhh. Tell me how old you are, Gabriella."

"Old enough, how old are you, Mr. I own my own architecture firm," she snapped back rolling her eyes insulted.

His eyes changed and he was suddenly very gentle. His hand moved to her chin and he moved his thumb from side to side under her lips. Her breath hitched at the thought of him kissing her again. Maybe she could be one of those girls who just hooked up with a guy for a night without expecting anything in return. Maybe she could get the hurt out of her head for one night and just have a good time. Oh how she wished he would gently kiss her. The first kiss had been full on passion and she had never been kissed like that before, but she longed for him to be gentle with her, too. Her thoughts were interrupted by his low soft voice.

"Well, as for my age I'm twenty-nine. Now, I'm trying to get to know you. You've complained because I had a girlfriend, which I didn't. I don't. You've complained that you have only known me for five minutes, when it's actually been several hours. I'm just trying to meet your demands, Miss Gerhart. Please play fair and give a man a chance," he pleaded with her moving his head closer to hers. He put both hands around her face. She closed her eyes and leaned her head up toward his yearning for him to kiss her.

"Oh no, Miss Gerhart. As much as I want your lips on mine again, we need to talk. I know you feel *this*. I know you want me. You have wanted me since I walked you down the aisle, but you don't trust me. You're hot and cold. One minute you are leading me on and the next minute you're pushing me away. Why don't you tell me? What do you want with," he mirrored her motion from earlier *"this."* His lip curled and he cocked his head to one side waiting for her answer.

Her jaw dropped and he could feel her body writhing beneath him. Oh yes, she definitely wanted him. He enjoyed the challenge Gabby was giving him. She pushed buttons he didn't know he had and she lit a fire of desire in him unlike any of the other women he had ever had one night stands with before. But, he knew his *M.O.* As soon as he had sex with her and the challenge was over, he would be ready for a new challenge. But, it didn't feel that way this time. For the first time in his life, he felt he was losing control because he knew from his earlier kiss he couldn't get enough of her. She had put him in a power struggle and no woman had ever done that before. He had pegged her for such an introvert. He had not expected her feistiness, but yet he found it such a turn-on.

"I don't know." Gabby put her head down breaking their eye contact and slouching in his embrace. He felt the desire leave her body. That was not at all the reaction he had expected. But, nothing with Gabriella Gerhart had been what he had expected.

"I don't have a lot of...well, experience. Again, guys like you hurt girls like me and I would rather not feel anything than feel that. You bring emotions back that I have tried very hard to never feel again. Yes, I feel it *this*. But..." His eyes sparkled as the stringed lights that had been hung for the reception and the glistening waterfront bounced off his eyes. This man begging for her body was so irresistible and beautiful. She was so frustrated and confused. She could barely think straight in his presence and he made her emotional. She said and did things she had never thought of doing before. He reached up and put one hand on the side of her face and she reflexively leaned into his hand so eager for every ounce of touch he would afford her. "But what, Gabriella," he spoke softly. "I can't give you what you want, what you need," she whispered. "And what do you think my needs are?" The band was now playing "Brown Eyed Girl" and the irony wasn't lost on him. He smiled looking into her hazel eyes. Even though the tempo was more upbeat, they still stood in a close embrace in a world of their own swaying from side to side neither unable to break their gaze.

"Um..." She thought for a moment if she should tell him she was a virgin. But, if she was going to be honest about what she couldn't give him, she knew she had to tell him. The thought quickly jumped into her mind that this would also be perfect for getting him to run away from her and relieving her of any more heartache. She felt sure that once he found out he would start laughing like he had earlier when she thought the model was his girlfriend and this time he would turn and walk away. The thought of him walking away from her was just as heartbreaking as staying with him and giving everything to him, just for him to turn around and break her heart. She was in a lose–lose situation. He would either have his way with her and leave, or he would leave without having his way with her. Either way, she knew that there was no way to escape the situation without being hurt by him. A tear came down her cheek. He brushed it away with his thumb and looked concerned.

"Shhh. Why are you crying?" His voice was even softer and he was being so tender and delicate with her. She didn't understand. She knew what his goal was. It was like every other guy. He wanted to get screwed by a cute college girl and then he'd go back to his life as big CEO and she would be left to feel like a cheap whore. Oh, she knew that feeling all too well. The thought of being used like that again made her angry and once again her emotions changed.

"I'm a virgin, Bradley. I know guys like you want to get laid with cute little college girls like me and then leave the next morning like nothing happened. I'm not a cheap whore. I don't sleep with the first guy who is charming. I can't give you what you need. Well, I could, but I won't. I'm not looking for a one night stand. I'm looking for...well, actually, before today, I wasn't looking for anything," she rambled at him and she was about ready to run away again, but his hold tightened knowing she would bolt after that comment.

"So, before tonight, you weren't looking for anything. Can I take that to mean now you are? What are you looking for now, Gabriella? Obviously, I will admit, much to my disappointment, you say *sex* is not an option. So I would like to know what it is that you want?" His head cocked to the other side and he had a sly smile. He found her so many things, and amusing was one of them.

"Nothing. I don't want anything." She put her head down again.

"That's just not true, Gabby. Tell me what you want." He tilted her chin up again to look into her eyes once more.

"I don't want to share any part of me with a stranger who is just going to walk away. With every touch, every kiss, every word, I give a piece of myself and to have someone take, take, take and then just walk away makes me feel like a piece of garbage that can be tossed out when...when I'm all used up. I would like for once for a boy, I mean, ahem, a man, to get to know me first before taking my body. I am more than my body. The next man I let get close to me will have to want my mind, body, and soul. I told you I can't give you what you need, and frankly, I don't think you can give me what I need, what I deserve. Are we done?"

Gabby couldn't believe she had just said all of that. But, she was tired. The emotional toll this day had waged on her body coupled with the wine made her just want to be in bed curled up with a good book before she dozed off to sleep. Maybe now he would finally let her go like she had tried to do so many times before that night.

"You're right," he spoke softly. She was unable to hold the tears back from her eyes any longer. She knew it, but why did it still hurt so bad.

CHAPTER 8

September 2007

"Ian, we have to talk," Gabby said seriously.

"No, what I have in mind doesn't require talking." Ian grabbed her by her waist. She was smiling as he trailed kisses down her jaw to her neck. He was moving her backward toward the couch. Unable to resist him, she resigned to trying to talk to him until after they had made out and had their fun. Why had she thought they could actually do anything other than *this* after spending all day in three different classes barely able to touch one another? It was nearly impossible for both of them to resist public displays of affection at school. *Yes, talking would most definitely have to wait!*

Gabby moaned as he gently laid her back onto the couch and hovered over her. Ian lifted the hem of her cotton shirt, "You're wearing too many clothes, I do believe." He barely stopped kissing her while he tossed her shirt on the floor beside them. It made her giggle as she grabbed his shirt and repeated his words back to him, "You're wearing too many clothes, too, I do believe." After his shirt was on the floor beside hers she reached for his button on his shorts.

She wasn't usually so bold, but Ian had been playful with her all day, from his silly note to the slap on the rear as she was walking into the house. Gabby's behavior surprised Ian and so for the first time since they had been together, he reached for her skirt, slowly pulling it down, never taking his eyes off her, silently asking permission. She smiled at him as she threaded her fingers through his messy hair and gave him a gentle nod of affirmation.

After he had tossed her skirt into the pile of their clothes, he added his shorts. They were half naked in front of each other and he looked her over from head to toe smiling and drinking in her beauty. It took everything he had not to continue undressing her, but he didn't want to push his luck. She pulled him down to her and he began to kiss her lips, sucking her bottom lip softly. Their tongues were dancing together, exploring and tasting each other's mouths. He moved his tongue to her jaw and then to the back of her ear and tenderly nibbled on the lobe around her earring. She gasped and tilted her pelvis toward him. She loved it when he did that to her ear. She could feel his smile as she started to move. His tongue moved to her neck and continued to explore her body. Ian raised his hand and gently removed her breast from the cup of her bra. She briefly looked down at herself and how trussed up she looked like that.

She was a little shy but she smiled as his mouth took her breast and swirled his tongue around her nipple making it harden and she felt all the blood rush down. As he pressed his erection into her panties, she could feel her wetness seeping through and she started to thrust her hips. He felt so good, *this* felt so good. She reached her hands to his back and moved her hands lower until she had his strong buttocks in both hands as he moved his kisses back upward toward her mouth again.

They began to really start moving in a synchronized rhythm and their kissing grew more passionate as she became more aroused. He stopped kissing her briefly as he smiled back down at her. He knew she was close. He loved to watch her as she rolled her eyes into the back of her head and how her mouth formed a perfect O as she came undone beneath him, all because of him. Knowing no one was home, she could not control her moans and she screamed out "Ian" as her orgasm spiraled all around her, shaking her body and making her limbs go limp.

Ian gently leaned down and kissed her for a few moments in a long hard kiss. Looking back up at her smiling he said, "Thanks for that anatomy lesson. I think I definitely aced that test." She rolled her eyes and giggled, "Yes, I think you should get extra credit for that one!" After placing her breast back into her bra, he handed her the shirt, "Hey Gabs, I did want to talk to you about something. I just, well, I couldn't think about talking when I first saw you standing at my door. You know what you do to me." She smirked, "No, I don't know what I do to you, but I do know what you do to me. I like it. I can't get enough. You bring out a side of me I didn't know I had."

"Oh, Gabby. That feeling is quite mutual. I am pretty sure you do to me what I do to you and then some." His voice cracked as he spoke almost shyly. He held her skirt out for her as she slipped each foot in and then he pulled it back up for her and then proceeded to re-dress himself.

"What did you want to ask me?"

"Yeah, John is having a party tomorrow. I know I had said no dates until we got to know each other. I think I'm ready to show everyone that you are mine. Would you like to go to John's party with me tomorrow night? Did you have plans?" He was hesitant as the words fumbled out of his mouth. It was obvious Ian was nervous.

She put her finger over her lip to try and hide her smile. She was so excited she almost started jumping up and down, but she loved seeing him so nervous and she decided to play with him a little bit in his vulnerable state.

"Actually, I do have plans."

"Oh. Okay. I guess I should have asked sooner. Maybe some other time," he said as he put his head down in defeat.

"I had planned to go to John's party with Lindsey. She asked me after school as I was leaving to come here. I wondered why you had not asked me. I mean, I knew we weren't technically dating, but I was disappointed that you had not at least mentioned it." Gabby was no longer playful, she was serious. It had really hurt her, but now she understood and she felt better. A slight smile brushed over her face.

"Oh. So you would rather go with Lindsey, then?"

Gabby cocked her head to one side and grinned, "Well, there's this thing. It's called a change of plans. Should I call Lindsey and tell her my boyfriend would like to take me to John's party so that everyone can see I'm his? If that's the offer, I won't be able to change my plans fast enough," she beamed.

"Yes, that's exactly what I want you to do!"

He leaned over and kissed her once more, "Pick you up at seven?"

"Yes, thank you, Ian. I can't wait. You have just made me the happiest girl on the planet. Want your reward?"

"Now you're talking!"

CHAPTER 9

June, 2010; The Present

Tears were streaming down Gabby's face. She felt like her heart was made of glass and someone had just shattered it all over the wood beneath her feet once again. She had known this guy for all of five minutes and he had already shattered her. *What was so wrong with her? Why was she never enough? Why couldn't guys appreciate a girl who didn't throw herself at every guy?* She began to get frustrated and she was so angry she contemplated slapping him as hard as she could, but she didn't want to be the center of a scene and she certainly didn't want to ruin Cade and Kristin's big day by slapping his cousin. She was paralyzed with emotion and as much as she wanted to run away from him again, she found herself planted in front of him wishing she was anywhere but there.

"You're right," he said. She had heard him the first time. Hearing it twice certainly was like adding salt to her wounds. He reached up and cupped her face one more time. She swiftly removed his hand and put it back by his side. "Don't. Don't touch me," she hissed. "Gabby. Hush." His voice was soft, sincere, but commanding.

"I'm not going to lie. I want you. I want all of your body right now.

I want to kiss that lip you're biting so soft and tender. I want to touch you and I want to make you come undone beneath my hands. I don't do commitment, Gabby. It's not who I am. I am really good at one night stands, the friends with benefits thing. I don't want to hurt you. I don't want to see you cry. I would rather tell you this than make you feel like a used piece of garbage. Please don't cry. Please let me have this night with you. Even if we can't meet each other's needs. Please let me just have this night holding you, dancing with you, looking into your beautiful golden eyes, Gabby. Please don't run away from *this*." His plea was sweet as he gestured that familiar gesture they kept mirroring to each other.

He raised his hand gently and slowly raising his eyebrows as it reached in front of their faces to imply what his intentions were and she didn't move. He continued and gently brushed a stray piece of hair behind her ears and he planted a gentle kiss on her forehead as she leaned her head down and ultimately into his awaiting lips. He moved his hands to the side of her face still swaying to the music and he used his thumbs to wipe away her tears. He pushed her hair out of the wetness brushing it behind her shoulders.

"I'm really tired, Bradley. Emotionally. Physically. I don't know if I can do this. As tempting as you are, the reality is that you're going to leave me. Even if I stay tonight, you're going to leave me and go back to your life and I'm going to be left writhing and missing your touch, your face, the way you make me feel with your commanding voice, and I don't even know you yet. I'll be left wondering what if. Your touch is painful to me if you can't want all of me. You can't just have my body." Her voice cracked as she spoke her last sentence and tears again prickled the back of her eyes.

He dropped his hands at her admission that his touch was painful. His lips formed a hard line and he clenched his fits. He realized the last thing he wanted to do was hurt her. What he really wanted to do was to grab her face, kiss her and make her forget all of this *baggage* she was so worried about. But, he also knew he didn't want to become new baggage. Bradley knew that even though he wanted her, wanted to worship her cute little body and make love to her, it wouldn't be enough. He knew that he wasn't capable of a serious relationship. The thought sent a pain throughout his body he had never experienced. He backed up to put some distance between the two of them. He certainly couldn't make rational decisions being so close to her.

Realizing he had been defeated, he put his arms up to surrender stepping back once more, "Okay. I don't want to hurt you, Gabby. I wish this could have been different. You're different. I don't want to let you walk away, but you're right. I will hurt you and I can't stomach the thought of that. You deserve better. I guess this is goodbye, huh?"

Tears streamed down her face. *Why was she so emotionally screwed up and unavailable*? She was furious with herself and proud all at once. She was five thousand emotions, whom was she kidding? She was a friggin' basket case, and that wasn't Bradley's fault. She was this way before she even laid eyes on him.

"Goodbye Bradley." She turned on her heel and walked away.

He froze in his position, with his hands in his pocket defeated as he watched her run to Sam, who held Gabby at arm's length. Her lips pursed and Sam looked up and scowled at him. She put her arm around her little sister and they ran into the Charleston night. Just like that, Gabriella Gerhart was gone and now a part of his past.

CHAPTER 10

February 2008

As Gabby waited for Ian to pick her up to take her to the Miss Penn Foster High pageant, she smiled as she thought back to how Lindsey had tried to talk her into entering the pageant, but Gabby was still too insecure about her figure to muster up the courage to compete. It was more than that, though. Lindsey's parents were rich. She could do or have whatever she wanted. Gabby was essentially an orphan. Her mother had left her father when she was five years old. Her mother had passed away the year before of breast cancer. Money was especially tight for her and she knew that not only she did not feel great about her body, but she also worried about how she would ever be able to compete with the elaborate evening gowns the other rich girls would be wearing. The bottom line was that even if Gabby had no issues with her body, she just couldn't afford to be in the pageant. There was no way she would admit that to Lindsey. Lindsey would ask her parents to pay for everything and then Gabby would just feel like she was a cause, something needing to be saved. She was low middle class, but she didn't want to be treated like she was living in poverty, she definitely didn't want pity.

Lindsey had pleaded, "Gabby, it will be so much fun. Who cares if either of us wins or loses? Let's just do it together. We'll get to go shopping for new dresses. We'll get makeovers. It will be so much fun. Please?" Lindsey drew out the last word as a plea while giggling as she nudged Gabby. Gabby was trying her best not to smile, but she couldn't help but smirk and laugh at Lindsey acting like a kid in a candy store trying to persuade her to enter some stupid high school popularity contest. Gabby rolled her eyes and let her body give into Lindsey's nudge. Twirling her hair through her fingers, she looked out the window as Lindsey drove to pick up John and Ian for their double date.

"Nope, sorry. I love you, Linds. I give in to you a lot, but not this time. I have absolutely *no* desire to be humiliated in front of the entire school and then some. I'm happy to come cheer you on, but I'm gonna pass on this one." Lindsey frowned, "I don't know why you think so little of yourself Gabby. You're beautiful. You didn't think Ian would care about a girl like you, but look at you. You're the girlfriend of one of the most popular guy in the school. You're not just beautiful, but you have the heart...the insides to go with it. You're the whole package. It makes me sad to see you so down on yourself all the time."

"Nice. Trying to guilt trip me into entering the pageant? It's a new Lindsey low!" Gabby giggled.

"Well, a girl has to give it her all," Lindsey snapped with a wry smile and they changed the subject to how in love they were with their boyfriends.

Ian knocked on the door snapping Lindsey out of her flashback and she quickly grabbed her cell phone, purse, cardigan, and slipped into her shoes. She took one more look in the mirror and fixed her already perfect straightened hair and opened the door with a smile.

"Well, hello there beautiful!" Ian smirked as he looked her up and down and wrapped his arms around her waist, "You. Look. Incredible," he said pulling her into a kiss.

"Oh, stop." Gabby blushed as she pulled away and looked down.

"Well, it's just the truth, Gabs. If you were in this pageant, no other girl would stand a chance," he bragged.

"Not true, but thank you. Let's go." She closed the front door and started walking toward his SUV.

Ian opened the door for her as she carefully climbed into her seat, "So, my parents are out of town this weekend. They left me at the house all alone. I promised I would check in with my grandparents every four hours and there is a chance they could pop up at any time, but I had plans for us. How long can you be out tonight," Ian probed glancing a smug smile over at Gabby as he put the car into gear, looked into the rearview mirror, and pulled into the street out of his parallel parking spot. "My curfew is the same as it's been all year, Ian. 11:30 p.m."

"Okay, good enough for me."

The rest of the drive, they chatted about the different girls in the pageant and how fun it would be to people watch the girls as they waltzed across the stage like mechanical dolls.

CHAPTER 11

August, 2010; The Present

Gabby had finished her summer semester making her usual 4.0 grade point average. She was thankful for a few days to relax before the fall semester started. She was taking a full load and she had put off most of her least favorite courses for her sophomore year. She knew this semester was likely to kick her tail. It was going to require more effort than usual. She had decided to go to Charleston to spend a few days at the beach and relax with Sam for the weekend. The sisters talked every day, but sometimes it was those moments when they were together, but didn't say a word that Gabby treasured the most. The moments when they just knew what the other needed and they were just there for the other. Gabby couldn't wait to be in Sam's presence.

Freshman year had been one of the best years of her life. It certainly had been better than her senior year. Gabby's last year of high school had been one of the worst years of her life. In fact, there were only two years that had been worse. The first, she was barely old enough to remember at the young age of five, the one when they had left her father. The second year was her sophomore year of high school. That year had been the year they found out her mother had breast cancer and she had passed away six months later.

The best part of the last year had been being close to Sam again. If it had not been for being close to Sam, she shuddered at the thought of what might have happened to her. She had been in a deep, dark depression and Sam had brought her back into the light. Sam had gotten her into the college nightlife. As much as she had hated parties in high school, she liked the frat parties in college. She loved being able to go to a house with a bunch of strangers and not feel the need to impress anyone. She loved drinking just enough to take the edge off her emotions and forgetting how badly she hurt. There was never a dull moment either at those parties. Most people were so drunk they wouldn't remember the stupid things they would say or do. Most of all, she loved that she and Sam were best friends. They shopped together, partied together, laughed together, and cried together.

Sam had settled back into their old house in the weeks after the wedding fiasco. Gabby had tried to block Bradley Banks out of her mind. She had spent all of her energy burying her head in her books studying. Sam was the only one who knew what had happened with him and she knew better than to ever bring it up to Gabby. Sam had hoped that Gabby would eventually break down and talk about what had happened, but she never did. She had just run over to Sam and begged her to take her home. She cried the whole way home looking out the window, but never told Sam what he had done to upset her so much. It had been one of those moments where Sam instinctively knew that just being there for her was what she needed.

Sam's summer had been busy watching television shows on HGTV and TLC on how to update the house on a budget. It was amazing at how the little projects that were so inexpensive could change the cozy beach cottage for the better. They were so thankful they didn't have to sell their childhood home when Grace had passed away, but it had been yearning for its own TLC in the years since her passing. Emma was kind to come to take care of Gabby, but she had not been the best housekeeper. It had taken Sam all summer to clean the place back up and each weekend she tackled a new DIY project.

The house was only a few blocks from the beach. It was a small house. Their mother had financed it with life insurance money from Sam and Gabby's grandparents when they were little girls. Grace had always wanted to live near the beach and she knew that the best way to invest her inheritance money was in real estate. The girls had loved growing up close to the water.

The beach had become therapeutic for them. The waves crashing and then receding over and over again, the feel of the warm soft sand beneath their toes, and the way the breeze blew through their hair were all feelings the girls craved when things hurt in their lives or when they just needed some time to reflect and relax. Gabby had walked up and down Folly Beach to the pier and back with a flash-light in her hand the night of the reception, letting her toes sink into the cool wet sand looking for shark's teeth and trying to think of anything but him. That was the last time she had been to the beach until today.

Gabby had called Sam and asked her to meet her at the beach when she got back in town. Gabby couldn't wait to sink her toes in the wet sand another minute and to just feel relaxed. She grinned as she fluffed her towel and put it down on the sand, placing her tote bag in the middle. She started to shimmy off her shorts and toss her loose tank top onto her towel. The beach was alive and the sounds of children laughing in the background made her heart warm.

She was on her way to the water when she heard Sam call her name and felt something familiar. Confused at her feeling, she turned around and her jaw dropped. Her eyes met his and she felt tears prick the back of her eyes. She wasn't sure what emotion had brought those to the surface. Were they angry tears? Were they tears of relief? No, she thought. They can't be tears of relief. It's not like there was anything to get over. They were nothing. They were one night of crazy emotions, crazy feelings. What in the world was he doing here? What was he doing with her sister?

Sam had stayed back to give them some space and fireworks went off in Gabby's body as he approached. She closed her eyes for a moment and opened them back up wondering if she was dreaming, but she wasn't. He was there and he was close enough that she could feel his breath on her face. She looked up into his blazing eyes and spoke softly trying to keep her emotions at bay, "What are you doing here?" her voice cracking as she softly spoke.

CHAPTER 12

February 2008

Ian and Gabby had taken their seats on the bleachers in the high school gym to watch the pageant next to the Martins. John and Lindsey were the cutest couple and Gabby had been pleasantly surprised at how easy it had been to hang around with John's family again. She had closed herself off after her mother had passed away and even though she had tried to avoid John, he had been nothing but nice to her. In fact, he had been the closest thing to a brother she had ever known. She couldn't understand how he was always so nice to her despite her distance to him.

Stella was sitting next to Gabby on the bleachers and put her arm around her shoulders giving her a warm sideways embrace, "Gabby, darling. I wish you had entered this pageant. There is no doubt that you would have won, but don't tell John I said that." Stella winked at their little secret. Gabby laughed, shaking her head disapprovingly, and playfully rolled her eyes. Since the pool party in August, Stella had become more of a second mother than Emma ever could be. Gabby loved Emma, but Emma had lost her husband and her sister in a year. Grace had asked Emma on her death bed if she would move to the beach and take care of Gabby until she finished high school.

There was no way Emma could have said no to her sister's dying wish. But, Emma had been despondent and emotionally detached.

Gabby was sure she was numb, paralyzed by grief. She understood. They had basically spent the year co-existing in the home. Emma made sure Gabby had what she needed, but she was not in a position to provide the emotional support that was necessary for a young girl losing her mother at such an important time in her life. Stella had invited Gabby and Lindsey over for dinner every week at least once a week. The Martins' large downtown home had started to feel more like home to Gabby this year than her own home had. The Martins' home was filled with good memories and always smelled of something fresh baked, whether it was bread or cookies, while her home had constant reminders of what she had lost, and lingering scents of things that constantly reminded her of her mother.

Gabby's thoughts stopped when she heard the older former Miss South Carolina who was MCing the pageant speak into the microphone, "Welcome ladies and gentlemen, boys and girls," and briefly pausing to nod down to the judges, "and our wonderful judges! We sure do have a special show of beautiful girls for you tonight." Oh her voice was annoying and Gabby rolled her eyes trying not to laugh thinking how fake this *beauty queen* sounded. *Yes, she was glad she had not entered this ridiculous pageant*, she thought. The MC introduced each judge. They ranged from college professors to local musicians. Each stood and turned to wave at the crowd as their name was called.

Next, terrible techno music started to blare through the sound system in the gym and the contestants walked out wearing their sportswear outfits, strutting across the stage as their names were quickly introduced. They were read by age, the seniors going last. When it was Lindsey's turn, they all clapped, laughed, and whistled as loud as they could to support her and it made Lindsey giggle as she walked up to her spot, her crystal blue eyes sparkling as the stage lights hit them at just the right spot.

Two hours later, Gabby was trying to contain her boredom. The only times she stopped yawning was when Lindsey was on stage and when she thought about what Ian had planned for her after the pageant. "And, the moment you have all been waiting for. Your 2008 Miss Penn Foster High is..." the pageant was finally over and the girls were all lined up across the stage holding hands in their designer evening gowns, large hair styles, heavy makeup, stilettos, and false eyelashes. The sight made Gabby laugh for a moment until she realized the entire gym was quiet except for her.

To Gabby, the girls holding hands were just another way pageants were so fake. Holding hands as if they were supporting each other, *no,* she knew better. To each their own was the theme in pageants. They were the cattiest, meanest things she had ever heard of and she was proud of herself for not subjecting herself to that extra drama. Besides, it gave her several hours to sit next to Ian holding his hand. The thought of Ian made her smile as they called, "Lindsey Howard!" Gabby dropped Ian's hand, quickly jumping to her feet bouncing up and down on the bleachers with elation at the announcement that her friend had just won. She gave Ian a quick peck and then Stella grabbed her into an embrace, as they all laughed, proud of their Lindsey!

About twenty minutes later, they had all gathered into the common area to wait on Lindsey to finish her pictures and gather her stuff. "Gabby, Ian. We're going out to eat tonight to celebrate at Ruby Tuesday. Would you two like to join us," Mr. Martin asked them as he put his arm around Stella's shoulders.

"Thank you for the offer, Mr. Martin. I had planned to take Gabby out to eat just the two of us for our five-month anniversary." Ian looked down at Gabby and smiled a slick smile.

She beamed and felt her face turning red and looked back at Stella. Politely and genuinely, Gabby replied, "Thank you so much for inviting us, though. I, we, appreciate it more than you know." Stella grabbed Gabby by the shoulders and looked into her eyes, "Gabby, you are most welcome. When are you going to realize that I, we, we all love you as if you were our own? You are very special to us. You're welcome in our home or out to eat with us anytime, my dear." Gabby's smile turned from polite to relief at the sound of Stella's confession. Even though Stella had given her no reason to feel otherwise, it was nice to hear that she was loved. Yes, Ian had told her he loved her in December around Christmas, but she realized in that moment, that since her mom had died, she had not heard those words from an adult other than Sam. She had not realized just how alone and in fact, unloved, she had felt for the past year and a half.

CHAPTER 13

August, 2010; The Present

"Gabby," Bradley spoke softly as he brushed a stray hair out of her eyes and tucked it gently behind her ear.

Gabby felt all the air leave her body and she couldn't help herself as she leaned into Bradley's hand. *Oh, his touch.* She had only known it for a few moments before she had ran away that night in June, but until she had felt it just then, she had not realized how much she had been missing it, how much she had longed for it. She felt her face start to redden and those familiar feelings of arousal came rushing back in as quickly as the wave crashing in the background. She slowly closed her eyes as she breathed in a cleansing breath. When she opened her bronze eyes looking up at him, she spoke softly, "How did you know I'd be here? What are you doing here?"

"I called Cade and asked him for Sam's number. I called Sam last week and asked her how I could get in touch with you. She told me she thought you would be back in town today. So, I cleared my schedule for the weekend. I'm staying at the Harborview Inn again. I had just pulled up to your house as she was walking out to come meet you."

Bradley's eyes were gleaming at her with pride, anticipation, nervousness, and excitement at his confession.

"Wow. Sounds like you went through a lot of trouble to find me. I don't know what to say. What can I do for you?" Surely, he wasn't coming for anything positive. Their only encounter up until now had been raw with emotion and by all accounts had not gone smoothly. *Why would he electively subject himself to that again,* she wondered?

"I have tried to get you off my mind for the entire summer. I can hardly look at another woman because she's not you. I know that we don't really know each other. But, I had to see if I saw you again, if I touched you again," he closed his eyes again and sighed "if *this, this feeling* would still be here." He opened his eyes, looking at her with a look of resolve and relief at his own confession. She knew what he was feeling, because she felt *this,* too. But, she had felt that before and she had been left so badly broken and shattered. She had just really gotten over that in June when she met Bradley and she knew with Sam being away this year she was not emotionally ready or available to trust a man again.

"Say something," he whispered moving that same piece of hair out of her face again and also stepping a bit closer to her. He was so thankful for that piece of hair. He longed to touch her again, but he didn't want to push his luck. When she touched him again, he wanted it to be because she longed for his touch, too. Not, because she was pushing him away like she had done months before.

"I don't know what to say. Thank you for coming." It was almost a question because she was caught off guard and she wasn't sure if she was happy he was here, or not. She glanced down fidgeting with her fingers. *Oh this was awkward,* she thought.

"Are you really thankful I came, or are you just being polite, Miss Gerhart?" A slight smile formed in the corner of his mouth.

"Just being polite, I think," she replied, still looking down, she briefly glanced toward him and back down again, never moving her head.

Cupping her chin between his thumb and his finger he tilted her chin up so she had to look at him, "Do you feel *this*?"

"Yes," she whispered.

"Good, then come to dinner with me tonight at the Peninsula Grill." His voice was authoritative, and it made Gabby feel uncomfortable. She couldn't decide if the discomfort was because she liked that tone, or not.

"Miss Gerhart, the last time I saw you, you had quite a mouthful to shout at me. You're really quiet today. Cat got your tongue," he asked amused.

"No," she smarted off at him slightly smiling and relieved to release some of the emotional buildup she had been trying to contain.

"No, you won't come to dinner. Or, no, the cat doesn't have your tongue?" He curled his finger up over his mouth and cocked his head to one side trying to hide his smile. Oh, how he had missed Gabby and her cute feistiness.

"Oh, just knock it off, Mr. Charming!" She tried to act serious as she was shoving his chest pushing him away. But, as she pushed him she couldn't help but let out a small playful smile. It turned into a giggle when his muscular body didn't budge even a little bit at her efforts.

"Ah, I think that's the second time you've called me charming. If you find me charming, the least you could do is accompany me to dinner." He winked and quickly added, "Don't think I overlooked that you never answered my question, either."

Gabby placed her head between both of her hands and started rubbing her temples as she squeezed her eyes. She could barely think around this cocky, controlling man and she felt like she was starting to get a headache from dehydration, heat, and the myriad of emotions that accompany Bradley Banks's presence. "It's just that you..." she growled and shook her head disapprovingly. "I what, Gabby," he asked pushing her to continue to speak. "You make it hard for me to think....you're exasperating...you're infuriating," she sighed. "How?" He cocked his head to one side again, completely serious. "I don't know." she said looking back down and once again fidgeting with her fingers. "I do. Based on what you said that night, I think you are scared. I think *this* makes you so scared that you're running from it. I get it. I was only slightly relieved you ran last time. I thought I would be better off without *this*, because *this* has already been far more complicated than anything I have ever welcomed. But, I need to explore it and I have decided that I'll do whatever I have to do to get to know you better, Gabby. But, you, I think you're confused because on the one hand you feel it. You already said you feel it. Your mind is telling you to run, but your body isn't. You don't want to explore this because if you do, you will have to feel something other than the numbness. If you're numb, you can't be hurt again. I don't know what the jerk did to you, but I've spent the past several months glad that I don't know his name. I, as I believe you said, have only known you all of five minutes, and I'm already protective of you. Don't run away this time. I moved too fast with you that night. Let's take this slow. Please, a date, a real date. Let me take you to dinner tonight? Let me get to know you." It was a plea this time, not a command. He softly caressed her cheek again knowing the effect his touch had on her. She didn't realize it, but he could feel her relax every time he touched her. He knew she longed for his touch and was ultimately comforted by it, even if it scared her.

Gabby gazed into his eyes amazed at his honesty and how well he could already read her. She had told him that she wanted someone to want her mind, body, and soul. Was this his way of expressing to her he was willing to try? It's not like he came free from baggage or was Mr. Perfect. He admitted he didn't do commitment. Surely, he wouldn't have come all this way and made such an effort to just get laid. She was sure he could have that whenever or wherever he wanted it. She shuddered at the thought of him with another woman.

"Gabby," he pleaded interrupting her thoughts. "Yes," she smirked, again vaguely answering his question. *Oh, she's playing now*, he thought, slightly relieved. He narrowed his eyes and leaned a little closer putting their foreheads together and moving that stray piece of hair once more behind her ear. "Yes, as in what do you want? Or, yes, I'll go to dinner with you Mr. Charming," seductively smiling at her.

Her plan had backfired because with that move closer, his eyes bold and dilated, and that contact, all she wanted was for him to kiss her soft and tenderly, like she had longed for once before.

"Yes, I'll go to dinner with you," she spoke so softly he could barely hear her and she looked at him with raw vulnerability and excitement.

CHAPTER 14

February 2008

I an opened the car door of the SUV helping her in because Gabby had chosen to wear a black miniskirt with a black scoop neck top. It had three-quarter-length sleeves and clung perfectly to all the right places. She had paired the outfit with black wedge sandals. The outfit made Ian smile because dressed in all black. She looked cute and sexy all at the same time.

"Thank you," Gabby said with a flirty smile. "You're welcome." He winked as he shut the door and quickly jumped into his seat. "So, you said you were taking me out to eat for our five-month anniversary. Where are we going," Gabby inquired.

"It's a surprise." He didn't turn his head and he slightly glanced in her direction barely taking his eyes off the road, but she could see his proud smile. *What was he up to?* she thought. It was already 9:30 p.m. and she only had two more hours before curfew. "Well, I'm sure wherever you take me, I'll love it. You could take me to McDonald's and as long as I'm with you, I am sure to be the happiest girl on the planet." She grinned at Ian and reached to hold his hand. When she had put her hand in his he pulled her hand to his lips and kissed the top of her hand. Then, he took her finger and gently sucked on it. She gasped and her eyes got big. That had certainly not been what she expected. Again, Ian never took his eyes off the road, but she could see in his profile that he was definitely smiling his most proud evil grin. "There's more of where that came from shortly, Gabby," he teased.

"Hmm, well I guess we should eat quickly so I won't be late for my curfew, then." She leaned in a little closer to give him a taste of his own medicine. She brushed her lips with her tongue making them moist and she leaned into his cheek. Ever so gently she smiled as she planted a long and wet kiss on his cheek. Ian gasped, "Hey, I'm driving," as he began to laugh with anticipation.

"I thought you said we were going out to eat?" Gabby was puzzled as they pulled into Ian's driveway.

"Well, you are going out to eat. You're going to eat at my house. I'm not going out to eat. I did say I was taking you somewhere special. I didn't lie. Surprise," Ian smirked at his carefully thought out explanation as he cut the ignition off and climbed out to open the door for Gabby. "Um, what are you up to, Ian? Your parents would kill us if they knew we were here tonight alone."

"Why are you whispering, Gabby? It's not like we're playing hiding go seek and someone might hear you. We're alone. I do have something special planned for you. Come on." He grabbed her hand leading her into the front door of his large brick home.

Ian walked over to the stainless steel French refrigerator and pulled out several boxes from A.W. Shucks. He knew it was her favorite place to eat in Charleston. He started warming their trays in the microwave. While he waited he got out two dinner glasses and filled them with ice. "Do you want sweet tea, lemonade, diet coke, or water," he asked sweetly naming all her favorite drinks. Gabby was leaning against the counter smiling, "Hmmm. You're full of surprises tonight. Why don't you pick for me."

"Sweet tea it is, then." Ian poured the tea into the glass and then filled his. He handed it to her and smirking, he tapped his glass to hers, "To firsts."

"Hmm, what firsts are we toasting to? You sucking my finger in the car?" She was feisty Gabby tonight.

"Mhmm, well, and I had some other firsts planned, too," he winked.

"What kind of firsts, Ian," her mood quickly changed. She was now anxious and worried. Ian had never pressured her to have sex. They had done practically everything else, but he had always seemed fine with not taking it further. He knew she was a virgin, but he had never acted like that bothered him. Gabby had promised her mother that she would wait until she got married. That was not something she was willing to back out on at this point in her life. She just couldn't. *Oh, I hope our night is not ruined by this*, she thought as she bit her lip. Having put her drink down, she began to fidget with her long fingers.

"Oh, I guess you'll just have to wait and see," Ian responded to her question she had briefly forgotten she'd even asked. "Ian," she spoke softly. "Yeah?" He never turned to look at her; his back was facing her as he got the food out of the microwave. "Um, you know I'm waiting until I get married to have sex, right?" She was apprehensive and nervous to discuss this issue. "Well, I had hoped that we could do that tonight, Gabby. Why do you want to wait? I mean, everyone's doing it, I think John and Lindsey have even done it. I have condoms. We love each other. It just seemed like the logical next step, taking our relationship to a new level. Don't you want to,

I mean we've done everything else?" The sentence rattled off so fast Gabby could barely think straight. Her head was spinning and she suddenly wasn't feeling so great.

She reached out to pull a bar stool from the granite bar, climbing up with her head down. Her hands were trembling. She was so nervous, her appetite had suddenly disappeared. *How could she have been so naive?* It was obvious in looking back at their night from the moment he picked her up what his intentions had been.

"No, Ian. I don't want to do that. I don't care if everyone else is doing it. I don't care if you have five hundred condoms. It's not about that. Yes, I love you. But, I don't need to do that to prove that to you, or do I," she was trying to be calm and not run for the door to sprint home. "What's your problem, Gabby? No, I guess you don't have to do it to show me you love me. I just would think that if you *did* love me, you would want to share this with me. I want you. I have wanted you for the past three months and I have tried to wait until I could make it special for you. I thought you wanted me, too. But, well—clearly, you don't." He was sounding more and more defensive, almost agitated.

"Ian, it's not you. It has nothing to do with you." Gabby was trying to reassure him. "Oh, I think you're wrong. It has everything to do with me." Ian was growing angrier with each word that came out of Gabby's mouth. Here he had thought of everything: Making sure they had the house to themselves, check. Making sure he had her favorite foods, check. Making sure the date was special, check. The one thing he had not planned on was for her to say no. He was so frustrated because he felt like he had been so patient.

"No. It doesn't. You don't understand. If this is the only thing you're interested in, the only reason you brought me back here, then take me home. I'm not hungry, anymore." Her voice quivered and black tears started to fall from the mascara she had put on her lashes before she had left home.

"Gabby, I'm sorry. Please at least stay and eat with me," Ian pleaded.

Gabby sat quietly at the bar with her head down wiping her eyes. Ian didn't say another word waiting for her reply, but he did reach over and grab a paper towel and hand it to her because he knew she was crying.

"Thank you," her voice cracked. She cleared her throat, "Ahem, I will stay and eat, but then you need to take me home when we're done eating." Glancing up for the first time in what seemed like an eternity, she stared into his beautiful green eyes. Oh, she loved this boy. She hoped she had not just ruined everything. If she had not made the promise to her mother, she probably would have let Ian have all of her. But, that promise was far more sacred than any boy ever would be.

"Good. I really did want tonight to be special, Gabby. I got your favorites." He handed her the takeout tray with a silver fork. "Thank you," she smiled appreciatively. "So, are we good?" He took his food from the microwave and grabbing a fork, moved over to the stool next to hers to eat next to her.

She was playing with her food because her appetite really had never returned. She still felt like she could be sick at any minute. "I don't know, Ian. Are we good, because, I'm not going to change my mind? If what we've been doing can't be enough for you, then I need you to tell me now. I already love you so much, but if you don't think it's going to be enough, I'd rather be hurt right now than to stay with you and my feelings continue to strengthen. I can't imagine losing you as it is."

"It was stupid of me to assume that eventually you would come around, I guess. I love you, Gabby. I'll wait. Eat your food." He leaned over and kissed her gently on the cheek, much like she had teased him in the car. She blushed and suddenly any interaction between the two of them felt uncomfortable and awkward. She took a small bit of her food and thought about what to say next. She had no words. All she felt was awkward silence. The only person she didn't mind sitting in silence with was her Sam.

"Ian?" She glanced over to him and put her fork down, "Gabs," he replied playfully trying to recover their earlier mood. "I am really tired. It's getting late. I really appreciate you going through all this trouble. But, I don't feel well. Can I take this home and eat it when I feel better? Can you take me home, please?" She was fighting back the floodgate of tears she knew would come when she was back in her safe place. The realization that her safe place was away from him now made her even more remorseful.

"Yeah, I guess I should probably get you home. Would hate to break your curfew and worry Miss Emma." She could hear the disappointment in his words. He sighed exasperated as he got up from the bar stool and started gathering their stuff and cleaning up the kitchen.

"Thank you, Ian. I do love you." She closed the box and slid off the bar stool. He gave her a quick peck, "I know. Me too." She stood puzzled. That was the first time she had ever told him and he had not said it back to her. She shook her thoughts and reassured herself. *You gave him an out and he didn't take it. He does love you. Look at all the trouble he went through tonight for you. He's just disappointed. You'll both sleep on these emotions and everything will be fine tomorrow.* She slightly smiled as she continued to reassured herself.

CHAPTER 15

August, 2010; *The Present*

Bradley beamed as she spoke the words he had longed to hear since he had arrived in Charleston that afternoon. *Yes, I'll go to dinner with you.* They were music to his ears. He tried to contain his excitement, but he couldn't resist any longer. He picked her up and he twirled her around looking into her golden eyes that were perfectly reflecting the sun. Gabby couldn't help but giggle as she wrapped her arms around his thick strong neck and held on tight.

"Put me down," she screamed as she beat on his back and tried to act offended, but she wasn't. She was scared, guarded, but offended was not an emotion she thought she was feeling at that moment. She knew that he wasn't going to back down easily if he had come all the way from Atlanta to take her to dinner, so she thought she'd just go and get it out of the way. But, she also knew these feelings that they were both feeling. She'd only felt them one other time and she knew the hurt that came with them. But, he was so adorable, Mr. Charming, indeed. He was so hard for her to resist. She remembered what that felt like last time, too, and she rolled her eyes trying to get all thoughts of Ian out of her mind.

"Okay, okay. I just am so excited that you said yes. I couldn't help myself. Sorry." He put his fingers through his dark hair and tried to calm himself down after gently steadying her back on her feet. "It's not like I said I was going to marry you. It's just dinner. That's it. Okay," she playfully scolded him. "Yes, just dinner, for now," he winked at her.

She cut her eyes down and grabbed her fingers nervously. She laughed a shy smile and kept her head down toward the sand. She glanced up toward him and smiled. Bradley was dressed in khaki linen pants with an untucked crisp white linen shirt. His sleeves were rolled up just below his elbows and the top few buttons were undone, his dark curly chest hair peeking through the V the shirt had formed. He had taken his shoes off and rolled the bottoms of his pants up when he had gotten to the beach with Sam. His black hair was blowing with the breeze and he was breathtakingly beautiful. The more she looked at him, the more she realized he was the most gorgeous man she had ever seen, "So, um. I was about to go for a swim. But, you don't exactly look like you're dressed for swimming, definitely not in the ocean." She let out a giggle under her breath at how overdressed he was for the beach as she continued. "I'd really like to spend some time with Sam. I'm only going to be in town for a few days. What time should I meet you downtown?" She was now looking back into his dazzling blue eyes. She thought the good thing about dinner was that she'd have at least an hour to just sit across the table and stare at his beautiful face without needing an excuse. She had prayed for eye candy the night of the wedding, and that prayer had most certainly been answered.

Bradley interrupted her thoughts, "No, no need to meet me. I know where you live, remember? I met Sam. I had gone ahead and made the reservation for six. Will you be ready by 5:30?" Gabby laughed and rolled her eyes briefly glancing at Sam. "What, what's so funny," he asked looking around. "Well, there's something you should know," she teased. "Uh, ok." He was definitely interested and stumped at what her confession would be this time.

"I'm habitually late. I'll be late to my own funeral. Sam knows this and she thinks I don't know what she does, but if we are supposed to be somewhere, she always tells me to be ready fifteen minutes before we're actually supposed to leave. Then, I'm usually ready on time. But, sometimes, that's still hard for me to do." She grinned thinking back with positive memories of Cade's wedding and her running out almost falling and breaking her neck trying to put on her shoes while Sam waited in the car rolling her eyes.

"Oh, I see. This is going to be a problem, then." His eyes were playful and his lips curled into a smirk.

Gabby's eyes got big, she didn't know if she should gape or laugh. He was still so hard for her to read. "Seriously?" She was known to be quite gullible. "Yes, see I'm often late, too. So, this could be a bad combination. But, it could be that we were made for each other?" He cocked his head to one side and slipped one hand into his pocket smiling. "Oh, um. I'm not sure about made for each other. I am thinking probably a bad combination. That's usually how my luck plays out," she frowned.

He pulled her face back up, "Hey, why do you always look away from me. I love to look in your beautiful eyes, Gabby. Don't be afraid, don't be sad, and don't think the worst. I've never been more optimistic about anything in my life. I'll pick you up at 5:15. If we're early, we'll just wander around for a few minutes until it's time for our reservation. How does that sound?"

Gabby wanted so bad to push him away the way she had done at the wedding, but he was being so stinking sweet to her. If she had been watching this play out on television, she would have been putting her finger down her throat making gagging sounds and giggling with Sam. But, every time she had done that, deep down she had hoped one day her Prince Charming would come and sweep her off her feet. Then again, she thought Ian was her Prince Charming and he had swept her off her feet only to slam her back down like Humpty Dumpty, breaking her into a million pieces that she wasn't sure could ever be put back together again. Well, even if she was able to put herself back together, there was no denying she would never be the pre-Ian Gabby ever again.

"Yes, that sounds wonderful." she smiled. "And, hey..." he was starting to walk away. "Yeah," he stopped and turned just the upper portion of his body. "I'm trying," she hesitantly spoke softly. His lips pursed together in a closed mouth smile that caught the sides of his eyes, which were as intense as the summer sun, "Me, too. I'll see you in a little bit. Enjoy the beach with your sister, Gabby." He smiled warmly, nodded at Sam and with that, she watched as he walked away from her this time.

CHAPTER 16

June, 2008

Junior year had been the best year of Gabby's life. She had not only had a boyfriend the entire year, but she had the boyfriend she had dreamed of having for the previous four years. Things with Ian had been mostly good, except for the awkward moment when he had planned a romantic night for her after the pageant in February and she had turned him down. She had worried that they wouldn't be able to get through that obstacle, but they had and they were stronger than ever.

Before John and Ian left to go to their yearly soccer camp in North Carolina, John knew it was time to let Lindsey know that the relationship wasn't working for him. John had thought long and hard about his decision. He had not discussed it with Ian for fear that he would tell Gabby and that Gabby would then tell Lindsey. Awkwardly, John had chosen to discuss the matter with Stella. Stella was gracious and understanding. When John told her that he had felt the relationship was moving too fast and had become too serious she paused and methodically thought of how best to respond to such a delicate conversation with her son. She was so proud he felt comfortable enough to confide in her.

"John, you're in high school, honey. I support you and Lindsey, but I support you more. Now is the time to be hanging out with the guys and just being carefree. I don't want you to feel like you are trapped into being with a girl because you don't want to break her heart. I admire you for being the boy who is concerned about hurting a girl, but you have to learn to do what is best for you. Ultimately, if you aren't committed to the relationship, you're not doing her any justice by dragging her along." Stella placed her manicured hand on her son's leg as she tilted her head sympathetically.

"Thank you, Mom. I think I know that breaking up with her is the right thing, but it's hard because I do care about her. I think she's a great girl. I just am not interested in this anymore. I just feel like she's more of a sister to me. I have known her for so long. It seemed logical to date her since Gabby was dating Ian. I thought maybe over time my feelings would grow and change, but they haven't. I do love her, but not like a girlfriend. I don't know. This is so weird talking to you about this." John looked up into Stella's consoling eyes and breathed a sigh of relief for having gotten all of that off his chest.

"Don't feel weird. I know it's hard to believe but I was a teenager once, not so long ago, well maybe it was a while ago, but it doesn't feel like it. Anyway, I think she will be hurt at first, but I think eventually, she'll appreciate you ended it sooner rather than later. You know before things get even more serious." Stella reached over to grab John's hand in hers and to comfort her baby boy. It made her heart pull apart when she thought of John's turmoil in having to make such adult decisions. No, he was no longer her baby boy, but yet he was, he would always be.

"I am so worried that we won't even be able to be friends anymore. I really enjoy being with her. She's fun. She makes me laugh. How do I salvage a friendship while breaking her heart, Mom? I am not sure I would even like me if I were her." John's voice cracked as he spoke the last sentence. He was really struggling with what he knew he had to do. There really was no decision left to be made, he had made it. What hurt was having to get the courage to actually do it.

"John, you must be honest with her and true to yourself. It's the way you go about it that matters. You don't do this over the phone. You go to her house and you look into her eyes. You let her see how upset this makes you and you beg her for her friendship. Then you give her some space. She's going to need some time, but I do believe eventually, she'll come back around." Stella's smile barely reached her eyes as she tried to be positive for John when actually all she wanted to do was reach over and pull him into her arms and rock him back and forth like she had done seventeen years earlier.

"Thank you, Mom. I knew I could come to you, as awkward as *this* has been. I love you so much." He was relieved and he was surprised at how much better he felt. He knew that it would be awkward but that his Mom would be able to make him feel better and give him the courage he needed to actually do what he needed to do.

John ran up to his room and quickly grabbed his cell phone and his letter jacket. Then, he ran out of the garage door to his Toyota Tundra and took a deep breath as he tapped Lindsey's number into the phone.

"Hey, baby. What are you up to?" Lindsey sounded so peppy and the thought of ruining her mood suddenly made John feel like he might vomit in his truck. This was going to be harder than he thought even just a moment before.

"Hey, Lindsey," John paused and then mustered the courage. "I need to talk to you in person, it's important. Where are you?" he inquired.

"I'm at home. Gabby's here, though. We were about to go shopping. Can this wait till later?"

"No, it can't. I won't be long. I'm glad Gabby is there." John muttered quietly, sighing in relief. If Gabby was there, that means she wouldn't be alone when he left and she would have a shoulder to cry on. He shook his head at the thought of also losing Gabby as a friend by breaking up with Lindsey. Would Gabby understand why he was doing this? Then he realized, if he lost Gabby, he could also lose Ian. He shuddered at the thought.

Lindsey's words reminded him he was still on the phone, "Okay, whatever John. See you soon. I love you."

"Yeah, me too," John lingered on the line even after she had hung up before closing his phone and tossing it in the passenger seat of his truck letting out a loud sigh and running his hand through his thick, dark brown hair.

Lindsey lived on a large estate, not in a neighborhood or close to the beach. They lived in an old colonial home. It looked like something from *Gone with the Wind*. The massive brick home had six large white columns, an oversized wooden door and porches on both levels of the home. In between each column were long windows on each side of the door with working shutters. There were three doghouse type windows for the third floor. The house perfectly represented old world Charleston and fit Lindsey's native southern parents, well. As John pulled up into Lindsey's long, oak-tree lined estate driveway, he meditated on what he would say to her and he glanced quickly into the rearview mirror and tried to reassure himself that he was doing the right thing. He took a deep breath as he combed his fingers through his silky, dark brown hair again. He closed his eyes, saying a quick prayer, asking for strength, courage, and peace in his decision.

Lindsey met him at the door just as he started to knock. She reached out to wrap her arms around his neck and kiss him when she realized he was standing before her not moving, as if he were paralyzed. His bloodshot eyes were vacant, tear-filled, and he looked tired and hurt.

"Hey. What's wrong? John. Hey. Please talk to me. What's wrong with you? I've never seen you like this before." Every moment John stood there not moving or talking made Lindsey's concern grow.

"Can I come in, Lindsey," he asked stoically.

"Yeah, sure. Sorry, where are my manners? I'm just worried about you, John. What's wrong, is everyone okay? Has something happened?" Lindsey's face was drawn and her questions were urgent.

"Everyone's okay. Let's sit." He motioned for her lush couch in the formal living room. He didn't want to go any further into the mansion because he wanted to be able to make a quick getaway to the door when he had said what he had come there to say.

"Okay," she spoke softly as she sat nervously.

"Lindsey, I don't know how to do this. I just want to tell you that I'm so sorry. I really do care about you. It's just that *this* is moving too fast for me. It's too serious."

"Seriously," tears started streaming down her face. "I don't know what to say. I'm shocked. Are you breaking up with me? Is that what was so important. You needed to come see me to break up with me?" The anger and disappointment she was feeling was palpable making him shudder.

"I am so sorry. Lindsey, I do love you. I meant that. I just realized that I don't love you like you deserve to be loved. I love you like a sister. I think you're fun and you make me laugh. I just have started to feel like you're my best friend, not my girlfriend. I don't want to hurt you, but I don't want to lead you on, either. You deserve better than that, Linds," he paused.

"I gave you everything, John. You had no problem taking that. Would you take that from your sister? Sorry, not buying it. But whatever! You're right. I do deserve better. Now, get out," she hissed.

"It wasn't like that, I tried Lindsey. I wanted to feel differently. I tried everything. I don't want it to be like this. I don't want to lose our friendship. Is there any way that you could find it in your heart to forgive me for this and still be my friend," he said apologetically.

"You have some nerve, John. No. I don't think that's going to work for me," she said angrily as she opened the door and stood back motioning for him to leave.

"I'm so sorry, Lindsey. I hope you'll change your mind." He walked out of her front door with his head held down. He felt relieved to have that off his chest, but it hurt nonetheless. He knew he had done the right thing. He sought comfort in knowing that and knowing he had the support of his family. Lindsey slammed the door as soon as his foot cleared the threshold making him jump. He paused looking back and a tear streamed down his face, knowing that even though she was angry, ultimately it was a cover for the hurt he had just inflicted on her heart.

"Lindsey, what is going on down there," Gabby screamed as she ran down the wide wooden staircase after hearing the door slam and Lindsey bursting into a full sob. As she ran down, she saw Lindsey curled into a fetal position on the couch in the formal sitting room.

"Lindsey." Gabby pleaded wrapping her arms around her and waiting patiently for her response. Gabby was so scared. All she could think about was her mother's passing away. Suddenly, scary thoughts flooded through her mind, thoughts of losing Stella, or Ian. She had always been a sympathetic crier, and she began to cry, too.

"Gabby, are you crying?" Lindsey her voice quivering, she took a deep breath and used the back of her palms to wipe away her tears.

"It's Stella or Ian, isn't it?" Gabby sobbed. "No, Gabs. Stop. It's not Stella or Ian. They are both fine. John broke up with me." Lindsey was confused, sad and relieved. She was thankful everyone else was okay and that Gabby didn't have to endure more heartbreak, but this was a moment when she was falling apart. Gabby had never really had to be there for Lindsey like Lindsey had for her. Just when Lindsey needed Gabby, Gabby was being self-absorbed in her own pity and worry.

"Oh." Gabby sighed with a slight smile brushing her own tears away. She didn't know what to say. She didn't want to seem happy that it was just a high school break up, but she was so relieved that everyone was okay. "I'm sorry, Lindsey," Gabby said sympathetically. "What happened, Linds. What did he say? I mean, I thought things were going so well."

"He said that it was too serious and moving too fast...that I had become his best friend and he didn't have those kinds of feelings for me. Said he loved me, but not that kind of love. I just don't get it. Jerk," Lindsey emphasized the last word and it made Gabby cringe thinking of John, loveable almost big brother to her, John.

"Linds, I don't want to take sides. You're both my best friend. I just think in a way that if he was feeling that way, as much as it hurts, you should be relieved that he ended it and didn't string you along.

I mean, I wouldn't want Ian to stay with me if he wasn't really happy, you know?"

"Yeah, I guess," Lindsey sighed. She was growing angrier with Gabby by the minute. She might have said she wasn't taking sides, but she sure felt like she and John had both conspired and arranged this and she felt like a fool. After all, he had said he was glad she was there. *What was that about?*

"I'm not in the mood for shopping, Gabby. I just want to be alone. Can I call you later?" Tears started to swell in her eyes again.

"Yeah, sure. I am so sorry, Linds. I'm here. When you're ready to talk, just let me know. I love you." Gabby reached over and hugged Lindsey. But, Lindsey couldn't help but feel for the first time ever that Gabby wasn't being genuine.

CHAPTER 17

August, 2010; *The Present*

"Gabby, what is going on with him? He called last week to see when you'd be home again, but I had no idea he would just show up like that. I promise. I had nothing to do with him showing up like this. Well, I mean, I was walking out the door when he pulled up and he insisted on coming with me. Gabs, there was absolutely no deterring him. I hope you're not mad at me." Sam was almost out of breath from running over to Gabby as soon as Bradley had left the beach and her ninety-nine words per minute confession.

Gabby smiled, "No, Sam. I'm not mad. I mean, I was definitely caught off guard and at first I thought I was mad. But, it's hard to stay mad at a man who has driven all the way from Atlanta for the weekend to see you and beg you to go to dinner with him. Oh, what in the world have I gotten myself into, Sam," Gabby sighed unsure.

"Wow. That's pretty impressive. What did you say? I thought after the way you stormed away the last time you saw him he would never come back around. Have you seen him since the wedding? The way you two were, it looked like there was definitely something serious going on between you two."

"No, I told him at the wedding that I was no good for him. I told him that I couldn't give him what he needed and he agreed. So, I left because I couldn't be near him knowing that." Gabby shrugged, rolling her eyes as she looked away and out into the ocean.

"Oh. But, don't you think this is impressive?" Sam leaned in and nudged her, "Clearly he didn't mean what he said at the wedding." Sam couldn't hold back her eager grin any longer.

"No, it's not all that impressive. He's loaded and he's used to getting his way with women. I think it's just a challenge. I'll entertain him tonight, but that's it. I mean, it can't possibly work. He's a CEO of a prominent architectural firm in Atlanta. If he's related to Cade, I'm sure his family is wealthy. He probably doesn't even have to work. He probably just does it for fun. He's a lot older than me. I'm just a student from a family with no money. Who are we kidding? This has *never gonna work* written all over it, Sam."

"Well, don't go into it thinking that way. Just enjoy your night." Gabby interrupted her, "That's what he said."

"Which part, not to go into it thinking that or to enjoy your night?" Sam grew a little more serious. "Well, basically to not think the worst about everything. That he was more optimistic about this than he had been about anything. He's a real charmer, Sam. He's good, very good at getting his way. When I'm around him, parts of me I didn't know I had surface and it disarms me and empowers me all at once. It's so strange," Gabby rambled. "Well, maybe he's not trying to charm you. Again, give him the benefit of the doubt. I could be wrong, but I don't think he would go through so much trouble if he wasn't serious. Where is he taking you, anyway? Did he say?" Sam sometimes sounded more like a mother than a sister.

"Peninsula Grill. Picking me up at 5:15. He said he had already made reservations for six." Gabby laughed thinking back to the less serious part of their conversation and the thought that at least she could be her usual late self with him and he wouldn't mind.

"Wow," Sam gulped and her eyes were wide and bright. "Wait. Why is he picking you up so early if reservations are at six? It's just twenty minutes away." Sam looked puzzled.

Gabby busted out laughing because she had wondered if Sam would pick up on the time. "I told him I'm habitually late and that I'll be late to my funeral, and that you always tell me to be ready at least fifteen minutes before we *actually* need to leave. So, he moved the time back because he's also always late. He said this way maybe we can both be ready on time."

"Hey! How'd you know I did that? What's worse is that you know I do that and you're still *always* late," Sam shoved her laughing. "Seriously, Gabs, he has gone all out. Please don't run away from him again tonight. Promise me you'll give him the benefit of the doubt," Sam lectured her.

Sam ducked and covered her head at Gabby's playful swat. "Knock it off, the whole mother-talk thing. Yeah, yeah, yeah. I'll go to dinner, but it's not going any further than that." Gabby was determined to not get into a serious relationship with anyone, certainly not this man who already rocked her to the core. Part of her was relieved to be in his presence again and the other part of her knew that the only thing good that could come from a guy like Bradley was heartache. She rolled her eyes at the thought that she had been absolutely unable to resist him. She had actually longed for him to kiss her standing there on the beach, but he didn't. He had been so gentle, so gently, so charming.

"Oh Gabby, when will you realize you can't just close yourself off to all emotion forever? Ian was one boy. A boy. Not all men are like that. I'm sure there is someone for you who will treat you the way you so deserve to be treated, little sister." The girls plopped down on the towel simultaneously knowing they needed to have a sister-to-sister chat and Sam reached her arm to the side around her sister's shoulder and squeezed gently.

"I don't know, Sam. It's not just Ian. I think I must attract this type of man. I don't remember much about our father, but he was no knight in shining armor, either." Gabby put her head down and began to play with her fingers.

"Gabby, Dad was an alcoholic. He was a sick, abusive asshole. I make it a purpose to not think about him. To me, he's dead. You need to find a way to bury him, too. The things he did to you before Mom left him were unthinkable. I know you don't remember them, but I'm sure they are part of why you're so guarded. I know Mom pulled you from counseling when you quit talking. She thought the counseling was making you worse and the doctors didn't know what they were doing. But, in looking back on that, I think you should start seeing someone again. Maybe the combination of Ian and Dad has been too much for you. Maybe that was partly why you have been so depressed this last year. Maybe it wasn't all Ian?" Sam sincerely pleaded with her sister.

Being nine at the time their mother had finally gotten enough strength to leave her father, Sam remembered all too well what he had done to Gabby. But, she had never felt like it was her place to make Gabby remember. Gabby had to make the decision on her own to revisit and deal with those things. Sam refused to be her counselor. She was her sister and it might not have been the right decision, but Gabby needed professional help and she was not the person to go there with Gabby. Sam could tell Gabby was taking in and processing what she had just said. She knew she wasn't going to respond. The few times that their father was brought up, Gabby rarely would talk. In fact, that she hadn't jumped up and ran away meant that maybe she might actually be considering what Sam had said. So given the opportunity, Sam continued, "Gabby, would you go see someone if I went with you? I feel bad, I know what he did. Maybe we could do it together. I'm sure I could find us someone at school that could do it for us pro bono and maybe on the weekends. You could come home. It would be nice to see each other more, I already miss you and school hasn't even started. I am sure it would help us both." Sam was literally thinking out loud. There was no filter on the words leaving her mouth at all. "You would do that for me, Sam?" Gabby looked up and over at her sister's adorable face, her words were soft and her voice cracked because her mouth was dry from sitting in the sun and not drinking.

"Gabby. There is nothing I wouldn't do for you. I can't believe you would even have to ask. You're my little sister. You're all I have left. Well, other than our extended family, which aren't here and barely know us. I mean, you're it. If it will help you get over this baggage you've been carrying around. If it will help you feel again. Then, yes. I'm willing to dig up all the resentment and infuriating thoughts that come with our father to help you." Sam smiled gently leaning her body in toward Gabby's and giving her a sweet nudge. "Okay I'll do it. Let me know when you find someone." Gabby was resolved, determined and relieved.

Gabby and Sam spent the rest of the afternoon at the beach lying out in the sun and walking on the beach to the pier and back sinking their toes in their favorite part of the wet sand. They barely said a word, they had done enough talking. At this point, just their close proximity was all they needed. They just enjoyed each other's presence, and the beautiful familiar surroundings that brought them peace.

They made it home at five past four and Gabby rubbed aloe over her slightly pink skin and showered. With her towel still wrapped around her partially wet body and her hair twisted in another towel on top of her hair, she put her ear buds to her iPod in her ear and started her Christina Perri playlist. Oh, how she could relate to those songs. She liked every song by Christina Perri. She could especially relate to "Jar of Hearts" and "Bluebird." Gabby loved listening to music after having conversations like she had at the beach with Sam and Bradley. It helped to clear her head and reflect. As she thought about what she should wear, she crooned away, and for the first time in a long time, she thought she might feel hopeful. She was going to start doing therapy with her sister. She knew it would be hard, but she knew she had to deal with all these deep-rooted issues. More than anything, she thought maybe if she did this, then she might become emotionally available again, and be able to have a healthy relationship, especially one with a man.

Her thoughts were interrupted when she came to the realization that she had nothing to wear. She had packed only casual clothes with the plans of hanging out with Sam all weekend at the beach. Sure, they might go shopping and out to eat, but there was no way she would have ever dreamed she would be having dinner at one of Charleston's most famous restaurants. She slumped down onto her bed and buried her head in between her palms and sighed. There was no time. Where would she go in such a hurry to buy something suitable for the occasion? There was no way Sam could help. She and Sam had never been able to wear the same clothes like most sisters. Tears began to flow, not because she was disappointed she wouldn't be able to go out with Bradley, but at the sad realization that this was her life. No matter what, she would always be the girl that was less fortunate. She was less fortunate in the wardrobe department, in the parents department, in the money department, and the love department. Her tears turned to sobs.

"Gabby, are you crying?" Sam's fingers curled at the edge of the door as she poked her head around into Gabby's old room.

Gabby looked up wiping the tears with both hands from her eyes,

"Yep, don't act so surprised. You know I cry at Hallmark commercials," she managed to laugh.

"Why are you crying, Gabs? I thought you were okay with this date. You know you don't have to go, although I think you owe it to Bradley and most importantly to yourself to get to know him. He's trying, Gabs." Sam had walked across the room, grabbing Gabby's brush on her way to her bed. She removed her towel from her head and slowly started to brush the tangles out of her naturally unruly curly hair.

"No, actually, it's not that." She shook her head disapprovingly rolling her eyes, "I don't have anything to wear to the Peninsula Grill. Why was I thinking I could even remotely try to fit in there, with that group of people?" Gabby's hands were gesturing in the air in her attempts to release some of the hurt and frustration she was feeling about her life.

"Oh, Gabby. I didn't even think of that when you mentioned where you were going earlier. I don't know what to do. I wish that we were the same size. You know I'd let you borrow something. Dang it. What are you going to do?" Sam was disheartened for her little sister. She was secretly pulling for her to be happy with Bradley. There was something there that she had never seen between her sister and a boy or a man. Even though Gabby had not dated much, really aside from Ian, there had been no real boyfriends. But, Sam had not seen sparks or reactions from Gabby like this with any other person at parties, school, well, ever. She knew enough to know it was special.

"I will just call him and tell him I can't go. I mean it's pretty simple. This is perfect. Now, I won't have to deal with this drama." Gabby tried to sound excited, but she felt a twinge of disappointment. "Yeah, there you go. Taking the easy way out. Do you even know his number to be able to call him?" Sam had always been the practical child, Gabby the impulsive child. "Crap! No. Grrr," Gabby snapped.

"Well, looks like you'll need to go ahead and get ready then with what you have and then you can explain that since he made his little plans without consulting you first, that he'll have to give you a rain check on the fancy restaurants and take you somewhere simple tonight. I think that is much more logical and what was it you said? Simple." Sam smirked as she mirrored her sister's words.

"Grrr." Gabby narrowed her eyes at her sister making Sam roll her eyes with a wry smile.

"I'll leave you to get ready, then." Sam winked and jumped up to leave before Gabby could smack her.

Gabby looked into her suitcase and realized this was a nightmare. The dressiest thing she had was a pair of linen capri pants and a white tank top. She put it on and decided to not put much effort into her hair or makeup, *what was the point*, she thought. Once he saw her, he would probably realize this was not a good idea. What could the two of them possibly have in common, other than both being late? Gabby walked back into the living room to chat with Sam while she waited. She couldn't believe she was actually ready early.

Gabby recalled on the way home from the beach that Sam had told her about walking out of the cottage and seeing Bradley climbing out of his silver Nissan 370z. Gabby heard the deep rumble from his car before she could even see it. Suddenly, she had butterflies in her stomach for the second time that day. This time, she wasn't sure if it was because she was about to see him or that she was so pathetic, she didn't even have an outfit to wear on the fancy date he had planned, even before she had agreed to play along. The doorbell chimed and she blinked quickly trying to gather her composure. She stood for a moment at the door and pressed her lips together to shine the lip gloss she had put on before she had come into the living room with Sam. She grabbed the door knob and realized her hand was shaking.

CHAPTER 18

August, 2010; Present

"Uh, hi," she whispered as she opened the door, totally embarrassed.

Bradley was dressed in a black pinstriped suit. Like his tux had been at the wedding, it was perfectly tailored and fit his body well. Like the tux, it was just tight enough to show his well-defined physique. He had been irresistible at the beach in just khakis and a shirt, but like this, she wanted to just drink him in with a straw. She realized her butterflies were butterflies at the thought of seeing him again. She knew she couldn't do a relationship with him, but she sure was thankful she had the opportunity to see his face again. *Ah, glorious eye candy*. The thought made her smile.

"Hey you. These are for you." He leaned in and softly kissed her cheek, exchanging the large bouquet of purple hydrangeas, orange roses, and white calla lilies into her arms. She gasped remembering the flowers from the wedding. *Crap*. Sam was right. He had put a lot of thought into this date. She knew she was in trouble.

"Gabby, you look incredible, I feel bad, though. I should have probably mentioned the dress code at the Peninsula. I'll wait and put these in some water while you change." He leaned in to grab the flowers back and pushed her hair behind her ears, like he always did when he wanted to touch her but not be too forward.

She leaned into his touch without even realizing it, she whispered shyly, "Right. Um, I thought I was coming to Charleston to hang out with Sam and be a beach bum the entire weekend. I didn't exactly plan for dinners at four-star restaurants and all. Sorry, I don't have anything that I can change in to....maybe this wasn't such a good idea." Gabby's entire body tensed as she said the words. Her mind was scared but her body wanted Bradley Banks. There was no denying the flurry of sensations that had rushed through her body when she opened the door and saw this handsome man standing before her, but she knew from past experiences, her body had a way of deceiving her. "Oh, that was pretty presumptuous of me to assume you'd have something to wear. How inconsiderate. I'm really sorry. I just thought...well, I clearly didn't. Good thing we're both on time tonight. Sam," he poked his head past Gabby's and into the living room, "can you put these flowers in some water for Gabby. We gotta go get her a dress before dinner?"

"Bradley," Sam nodded. "Sure. I'll take them. This is a warning. The last time you were with my sister downtown, it didn't end so nice. Be good to her, please. She best not come home crying again tonight, got it?" Sam's tone was a bit protective and almost threatening. Gabby was embarrassed, but also amused. First, what did Sam think she would do to him? He was way bigger than either sister. And two, that Sam felt the need to act the role of both absent parents, helpful smitten mother and threatening father. Bradley smirked, "Got it. Thank you. I promise to take good care of her."

Smiling ear to ear, he took Gabby's hand and pulled her out the door. He opened the passenger-side door and helped her into the gray leather seat of his silver 370z, just as Sam had described it. This was arguably the nicest car Gabby had ever stepped foot into and it made her feel even more inadequate. *What did Bradley Banks want with a girl like her?* He shut the door after he made sure she was in good, and walked to his side. He climbed in swiftly. Glancing over at her as he did, "So, I don't know much about you. I know you like Christina Perri, but what other kind of music do you like?" She turned her head shocked that he had remembered her saying she had liked the song "A Thousand Years" at the wedding, "Colbie Callat, Dave Matthews, you know, the like. I am not picky, though. Whatever you'd like is fine," she stated shyly shrugging her shoulders non-committedly.

He smiled and pushed a button on the dashboard, "Well, I happen to really like this song at the moment." He looked over and smiled his charming smile at her as The Frames, "Falling Slowly" began to play in the cars Bose audio system. "Hmm. Interesting song selection, Mr. Banks. I do love The Frames," she mused. In that instance, Gabby felt herself relax in the playful mood Bradley seemed to bring out in her.

"Where are you taking me?"

"Shopping."

"Well, I know you said we were going to get a dress, but where?"

"Well, I thought we'd stop by Saks. They'll fix you up pretty fast. What are you, a size ten," he asked.

"Saks! That's a bit much, don't ya think? And, um, I am not going to ask you how you knew what size I am." She tried to hide her smile as she looked out the window. She could feel her face begin to blush. He obviously had far too much experience with women if he could look at a girl and figure out her clothes size. This could not be good, but she admitted to herself finally, there was nowhere else she wanted to be than with him at this moment.

"Reservation for two, Bradley Banks," he spoke authoritatively to the maître d'.

"Ah, yes. Please follow me, Mr. Banks," his posture had heightened and he was grinning as if trying to impress Bradley.

Bradley, holding Gabby's hand, led the way to the outdoor private dining area. It was breathtaking. One table centered in the middle of a lush courtyard. There were several balconies overlooking the area. Trees with heavy green foliage were surrounding the space. There was a rectangular stone water feature beside the table. The table had a large vase of the same flowers Bradley had brought to her earlier.

Even though it was usually extremely hot in August in Charleston, a cool front had passed through the area the day before making it more pleasurable to be outside. There was also a nice breeze blowing, but not too much. Bradley pulled Gabby's chair out and motioned for her to have a seat by putting his hand out palm up in front of him pointing to the chair. As she released his hand and sat down in her seat he moved her hair back behind her shoulder and whispered in her ear, "I love that dress. I love the shoes. I love everything. You look sensational, Miss Gerhart." She couldn't help but blush. He was so, well, charming. Even though she was scared and reserved, she had forgotten how wonderful it felt to hear that she looked nice from a guy. She had forgotten what it felt like to feel these magnetic feelings. They felt good and she wanted badly to forget the hurt she had been through, and just give into them, but she knew she couldn't.

The waiter promptly was at their side as soon as they had made themselves comfortable in their seats. Rather than asking what they wanted to drink, he had a bottle of champagne and he immediately began filling their glasses. When he was finished he placed the bottle in a silver wine carousel wedging the bottle in between the ice cubes.

"Rather presumptuous, aren't you? What kind of champagne is this?" Gabby picked up her glass and smiled a wry smile as she took a sip. "It's Champagne Perrier—Jouet. 2004 Belle Époque Rose."

"That's a mouthful," she teased. "Pun intended."

"Yes, it is a quite a mouthful in more than one way. Do you like it?" His eyes narrowed and his smile was seductive. He curled his finger over his mouth and gently brushed his finger along his lower lip as he appraised her as she took another sip. "Yes, it's delicious. I've never had champagne that tasted so good in all my life, but then again, I can only imagine the price tag on this bottle and so that doesn't surprise me that I've never had it. We, um…we live two totally different lifestyles." Her smile faded and she looked down at her fingers in her lap and started to fidget. "Well, you're young, Gabby. I've never really been interested in someone quite so young. I've always just been interested in women that were at the same point in their lives as I was, who didn't want a commitment. I don't expect you to be where I am. It will come, though. I'm sure you'll be successful in whatever you do. Cade says you go to Columbia College."

"Well, I don't know about all that. Hmmm, you've talked to Cade about me, huh," trying to change the subject from their social incompatibility, her eyes brightened and the mood had been temporarily restored.

"Yes."

"Is that all he said about me, that I went to Columbia College," she asked flirtatiously.

"No."

Narrowing her eyes back at him, "You're being monosyllabic, now, huh?"

"Yes," his expression never changing, still with his fingers curled on his lower lip, eyes narrowed and that seductive smile. "I suppose I am." He started to bite the side of his lip as he continued rubbing the bottom of his lip and it was obvious he was partially thinking about what to say and partially teasing her. Then he moved his hand away grabbing his glass. He leaned back in his chair taking a sip, shrugging his shoulders, "You know, we just talked. You happened to come up, that's all."

Gabby had leaned forward as he had leaned back, narrowing her eyes with a half smile, "So, you just happened to be talking to Cade and I just happened to come up in conversation. Right," she was sarcastic, rolling her eyes. She threw her head back with a laugh, like she had done at the reception.

It was becoming harder for Bradley to contain his grin. He loved watching everything about her. She was a mystery to him, but her every move made him want to embrace her and kiss her passionately as if his life depended on it. It was taking all his self-control not to do just that. He had made up his mind he would take things slowly with her. She had run away once before and he wouldn't allow that to happen again. But, he knew he had to make her realize that there was something there that was yearning to be explored.

"Persistent little thing, aren't you. No fooling you. Okay. So, when I called Cade to get Sam's number, I asked him to tell me more about you. You know where you went to school, how old you were. I just don't want to get myself into any trouble. I know you were drinking at the wedding, but I just wanted to make sure you were *old enough*." He repeated the words she had told him at the wedding about her age. "And, as it turns out, you're not old enough to be drinking, but this is private dining, so I took care of that whole situation."

"Oh, but you still asked. So you didn't believe me. Right. Because I was clearly trying to hide my age to seduce *you* and have sex with *you* as a minor. No, if I recall, that would that would have been *you*. Give me a friggin' break." She couldn't control the harshness of the comment, she felt like he was patronizing her about her age again. Again, in too many ways they were just too different. This would never work.

"No, you were certainly not trying to seduce me, more like trying to wound my ego, break my heart, I dunno. Did you like how you felt when you walked away? Do you prefer that emotion to *this*?" He smirked as he cocked his head to one side throwing his glass of champagne back and finishing off his glass. He motioned for the waiter to bring a refill. "Well, I doubt very seriously I broke your heart in the five minutes I knew you, being a bit dramatic, eh? Now as for wounding your ego, now that I would believe." She grinned and put her head down only slightly embarrassed, but also proud of the feistiness he brought out in her.

The waiter refilled their glasses and then brought their appetizer, Lobster 3-Way. "I hope you like seafood," Bradley grinned. "Actually, I am allergic." Gabby tried really hard to keep a straight face. She wished she had been videotaping his response to her comment. He nearly spewed his drink across the table at her, or maybe he looked like he might choke. She had mercy on him and put her hand over her chest diagonally as she busted out laughing. "Just kidding, geez, don't choke over there! Again, it was mighty presumptuous for you to assume that I liked seafood. You know, a lot of people can't stand it or really are allergic to it. Actually you presumed a lot of things, didn't you," she grinned. "I can order something else if you don't like it. I'm so sorry. I don't know what I was thinking. I just wanted to show you I had put a lot of thought into this. I told you I don't really do dates, serious relationships. I told you at the beach, though—I'm trying." She couldn't let this go on any longer, he was being so sweet. "I don't get to eat a lot of lobster, but I do love seafood in general." She extended her fingers to where they met his on the table and when they touched she felt as though she had been shocked, the electricity from his touch was so intense and she craved more. "That wasn't very nice, you know! Your little stunt." He was trying to sound wounded, with a seductive smile and narrowed eyes he let out a slight laugh as he shook his head from side to side, falling not so slowly for the girl across the table. With every word that came out of her mouth, he grew more fond of her. "I'm sorry. I couldn't resist," she tilted her head and her smile curved to the side as she blinked her eyes in an innocent way. She lifted one shoulder up as her head went in the opposite direction. Reaching over, she placed a piece of lobster ravioli on her plate and cut a small bit. "Mmmm," she murmured as she closed her eyes tight, a slight closed smile escaped as she savored the succulent taste of the delicious appetizer. Bradley watched her with amusement, "You like, huh?"

"Oh, yeah." She opened her eyes and brightly smiled at him.

The two playfully flirted through dinner. The moods had relaxed and there were undertones of want and desire. Gabby enjoyed herself, but she knew this would never work out between the two of them. But, she couldn't help but feel relaxed at how the conversation had been so easy.

They discussed her desire to do philanthropic work, although she knows she also needed to have a skill that will make her a living. Bradley told her how he had quickly climbed the ladder of success to the top and his passion for design was evident as his eyes lit up talking about his work. She was genuinely interested and she smiled back at him with her undivided attention relaxing back in her chair.

They had also shared low country oyster stew with wild mushroom grits as their first course. Their main course was her favorite, a pepper seared New York strip "Au Poivre." It was served with a crispy potato cake, teeny weeny benne beans, which were as good as they were adorably named, and it was all topped off with a Brandy pan sauce.

She learned through conversation that Bradley had come earlier and dropped off the flowers and the champagne and had given the chef their menu order. She realized this must have been when he also resolved the age issue, which had been the only real uncomfortable part of the conversation. He had planned every detail. Gabby thinking of the effort he had gone through to spend an evening with her made her feel like a princess. But, she had been treated like a princess before. Her subconscious always brought her back to reality and reminded her of the pain she had just gotten over and to tread carefully. People change. Sometimes, no matter how much fun you have with someone, it's just not enough. Interrupting her thoughts, "Hey you, do you want dessert here or do you want to go somewhere else?" He could tell she was deep in thought about something. He hoped it wasn't that she was having second thoughts about them. He really had been looking forward to dessert all night, no all day. "Hmm, I'm really full. The thought of another bite of anything makes me want to crawl into my bed and sleep off this full belly," she sighed as she splayed her hand across her tight black dress that he had chosen for her earlier in the evening when he learned she had not been prepared for the dress attire of the evening. It fit more tightly than she would have ordinarily chosen, but he was paying for it and he insisted that she get it. His burning blue eyes had given away that his words were truly what he felt and he made her feel so comfortable in her body. For the first time in her life, she thought she might actually feel sexy. "Well, they have world renowned coconut cake here. I really wanted to feed that to you. I'm sure you don't get fed like that at college. Perhaps, I could talk you into us getting a slice or two to go. We could eat it in a little bit after our dinner has settled. What do you say?"

"That would be nice," she was relieved. Bradley motioned for the waiter and he brought a box with two slices of the famous coconut cake with a side of strawberries. It looked divine and she couldn't wait for her stomach to make some room for the cake. He had said he wanted to feed it to her. She dismissed her thoughts of him slowly slicing a bite of cake with a fork and feeding it to her as if he wanted to care for her every need. *Snap out of it, Gabby!*

Bradley stood and offered her his hand for her to rise to leave. "Um, we haven't paid yet," Gabby spoke softly, more of a question than a statement. "It's already been taken care of, Gabby." he gazed down at her never letting his eyes leave hers. "Oh, okay." She placed her small soft hand in his and used her other hand to smooth her dress. *Makes sense, he took care of that with everything else. Duh, Gabby.* Her expensive heels were much taller than she was used to wearing and she was thankful for his hand and his arm because she was sure if he didn't help her, she'd fall walking through the cobblestone streets of Charleston.

"Where are we going now," she asked as she tilted her head up so she could see him. "Well, I thought we could walk around and visit some shops. Then I wanted to take you back to where we met and see if we could end our night differently this time." He glanced down and smiled at her eager to see what she would say to his plans. "Well, I suppose we could try that. Just don't be such a jerk this time. Oh, and you're going to have to keep holding my hand or I may end up breaking my neck in these shoes," she giggled.

"Oh, I think I can manage that for you, Miss Gerhart, the hand holding. And, a jerk. Ouch, that hurts. I wasn't trying to be a jerk. I didn't want to hurt you, and I'm sorry if I did. That was never my intention." Gabby glanced up at him smiling. She nodded and shrugged one shoulder, like she often did when she felt shy. It was her way of saying okay without speaking a word.

They strolled through the shops around the market, sharing with each other what they liked and didn't like. They laughed at other people and tried to figure out what they were thinking. Bradley had done a good job distracting Gabby from any thoughts of running that she had briefly entertained. In fact, Gabby felt so comfortable with Bradley. It was as if she had known him forever. He felt familiar already and they really barely knew each other. They wandered the street of Charleston arm-in-arm and Gabby couldn't shake the electricity that was beaming through her body from his touch, from his close proximity. It turned out that even though they were so different, conversation came easily.

Bradley had one more surprise in store for her before he took her back to the harbor. As they approached a white-horse-drawn carriage with a driver in a top hat, he stopped and motioned for her to climb aboard. She looked up at him in surprise as she smiled, "Seriously?"

"Yes, I thought it would be nice for you to have a seat. Those heels must be killing you and I wanted to take in the city with you," he grinned. "Nice," she said as she climbed aboard.

They rode through the city and the driver told them about the rich Charleston history. The tour also included the First Baptist Church they had met in just a few months before. She remembered how they had taken horse-drawn carriages from the church to the reception. It was at that moment that she realized he had not only put careful thought and consideration into his date, but Bradley Banks had made an effort to start over with her, recreating the night they met. The difference between the two nights was he was far more respectful. He had done this to show that he could be the gentleman she deserved. He had listened to her, talked with her. He had touched her, but only lovingly and she wondered if this was his idea of mind, body, and soul.

Even though the guarded part of her mind was telling her to not get close to him, her body told her much differently. Gabby decided to enjoy the night for what it was and deal with the thoughts in her mind later. She knew this could never work, but she had enjoyed herself so much. Bradley had taken care of every little detail to try to make the night perfect, she didn't have it in her heart to ruin it with talk about why this wouldn't work. She quickly dismissed the unpleasant thoughts and moved in a little closer to his side, it felt so natural and comfortable. As she did, he stretched his long muscular arm around her shoulders and she nestled herself into his side and inhaled his scent. She wasn't sure what kind of cologne he was wearing, but the smell was familiar from that night. In fact it probably wasn't just one thing, but perhaps a combination of aftershave, cologne and deodorant. She would often smell fragrances at the mall and she was sure she had never smelt anything so heavenly in a bottle.

As they neared the harbor, the horse slowed and she looked up into his crystal blue eyes, once again sparkling off the water and the moon. He put her chin between his thumb and his finger and pulled her face closer. He was slow and gentle, unlike the last time. He moved his head to hers, taking her lips to his and kissed her in a way that pleasantly took her breath away. Gabby felt her entire body squeezing her and she closed her eyes savoring his taste and the romantic moment. Even though she was torn between her mind and her body, her body was definitely winning.

Gently pulling back, but still holding her chin he softly spoke, "Do you have room for that coconut cake yet?" She could barely talk or think about anything other than what had just happened and how she didn't want to do anything but that again. "That was delicious, I mean that sounds delicious." she winked at him as they exited the carriage. He shook his head grinning, "It was indeed, Miss Gerhart. There's more of where that came from, that is if you want it."

They found themselves a swing. Bradley sat sideways on the swing so he could face her. She crossed her legs so her legs dangled while the swing swayed with the wind. He pulled out the slices of cake they had taken with them from the Peninsula Grill earlier that evening. There were two plastic forks. He opened one and Bradley proceeded to slice through the moist slice of cake and dipped the fork into the strawberries.

"Close your eyes," he politely ordered and she complied.

"You are beautiful, Gabriella. Have I told you that before?"

"Thank you, but I think you're the beautiful one," she smiled opening her eyes.

"Close your eyes, Gabby."

She was hesitant, "Just do it. Trust me," he said and she complied this time.

"Now, open your mouth."

When she did, he placed the slice of cake he had cut slowly into her mouth. He watched her reaction as she closed her lips and hummed as she chewed the slice of heaven. She had not swallowed all of it and she spoke with a little bit of cake still in her mouth.

"Oh. My. Gosh. That. Is. So. *Good*," she emphasized the last word.

"Mhmm. More?"

"Yes, please. Can I open my eyes, though?"

"No, it will be better with your eyes closed. You know, take away one sense, heighten the others," his tone was very nonchalant, but his grin was from ear to ear and he was certainly enjoying drinking in her beauty as she sat there waiting on him to feed her more with her eyes closed. Her long eye lashes were splayed on the tops of her cheeks.

"Okay. Makes sense, but aren't you going to eat any?"

"Sure, you can feed me mine after I've fed you yours first. Ladies, first, right? Hush now, open up."

Gabby couldn't say a word, she just giggled at the thought of feeding this gorgeous specimen of a man cake, sitting in the middle of the harbor on a swing. If anyone had told her in June before Cade's wedding this is what she'd be doing, she would have laughed hysterically at them. The only thing that made her more happy and eager was the thought of kissing him again.

"What's so funny," he asked concerned but still a bit amused at her sitting there with her eyes closed laughing, mouth full of food.

"Um, nothing. Sorry."

"Oh, no. You don't get to do that. Are you laughing at *me*, Miss Gerhart?"

"Nope, Mr. Banks. I wouldn't dare." She was over serious.

"You don't want to feed me my cake," he asked as if all of the sudden he was shy and sad.

"No. Yes. Ugh, not this again. Stupid mind and mouth are not coordinated tonight. I guess I should be thankful my mind and my feet are, though," she laughed and shook her head at her usual clumsiness.

"Well, I think your mouth was quite coordinated earlier. And as for your feet, I'm not going to let you fall. I don't want you to get hurt," he spoke softly as he moved a piece of hair behind her ear like he had done so many other times before.

She leaned into his touch realizing how much she was longing for every little touch he was willing to offer her. She had been in love only once before and that had resulted in such heartbreak, but she couldn't remember ever feeling like this about Ian. She shook her head trying to get Ian out of her head during this wonderful night. She couldn't let him ruin this for her.

"What's wrong. I'm sorry, Gabby. I'm trying not to be so forward, but I couldn't help myself. You're just…"

"No, it's not you. It's just I'm really trying not to think about getting hurt. But, I can't help myself. You've done all of this. I mean, the beach, dinner, the carriage ride, the harbor—*this*, it's incredible. I've had one of the best nights of my life. It's been so much better than the first night we were here, but the one thing that hasn't changed is the reality that when this night ends you'll go back to your life in Atlanta. For goodness sake, I'm a sophomore in college. This just won't work. When you touch me, I feel alive. I love your touch. I love just being with you. You were wrong earlier at the beach when you said I was scared. I'm not scared, I'm terrified. I can't go through this hurt again. I mean, how in the world would a relationship ever work?" Tears started to prick her eyes and she put her head down. "I'm so sorry. I've tried all night not to think about this and to just enjoy everything. It's been amazing. I'm so sorry. I didn't mean to spoil it. But, Bradley, that's what I do. I spoil everything," she confessed.

"Well, I think we've made progress, actually." He had not moved his hand from her face and he was gently stroking her cheek and he moved his thumb up to wipe the tears that were forming in her eyes.

"How do you figure that?"

"Well, you haven't run away. I think that's progress, don't you? You've admitted that you feel this. You're not denying that anymore." He had a half smile and he turned his head to one side looking into her eyes waiting for her response. "This is true. I don't want to run, but I don't want to be hurt either. I don't see how this is ever going to work."

"Gabby, we could live in the same town and there are the same possibilities of you getting hurt, heck, of me getting hurt. You're just looking for excuses because you're scared. I'm scared, too. This is definitely not my comfort zone. But, Gabby the moment I saw you I knew there was something special. I have spent the last several months trying to get your face out of my dreams. I've spent the last several months trying to be the person I had convinced myself that I was. None of that worked. The way I see it, I don't have a choice but to try this. The alternative to me is far more painful," he pleaded.

She closed her eyes and pondered his words. *The alternative to me is far more painful*. Was that true for her, too? She wasn't sure. She needed more information, "You have said you were quite the playboy back in Atlanta. I told you at the reception that I am a virgin. That's not going to change after a few dates. Is that something you can deal with? It shouldn't be something you think that I'll budge on if you swoon me and feed me with my eyes closed, you know, take me on enough romantic dates and she'll eventually give in this time. Waiting until I get married is something very important to me." She closed her eyes remembering her last conversation with her mother. Her mother knew that Gabby wouldn't have anyone there for her as she went through those difficult years in high school. She would be far too emotionally hurt from her death to deal with the emotions that come with being sexually active. The last thing her mother wanted for Gabby was for her to get pregnant and ruin her bright future. Besides, being Southern Baptists, premarital sex was highly frowned upon. Gabby's decisions to honor her mother's wishes had not been easy and she knew if whatever

this was with Bradley continued, it certainly would not get any easier. She was already having trouble resisting the urge and her
thoughts were certainly all heading south with every moment she
spent in his proximity.

"So, yeah, I knew you were a virgin. Waiting until you get married,
huh?" His eyes got wide and one of his eyebrows arched in his surprise. "Yes, that's exactly what I said. It's not up for negotiation,
either." She was firm and short. "Wow." He ran his fingers through
his hair as he looked away from her for the first time and broke
their touch. "See, I told you. This is not going to work. Can you just
take me home?"

"No. I'm not letting you get off that easy this time. I should have
gone after you last time. I am certainly not going to condone your
running from me as soon as things get a little intense."

"I'm not running. I'm being realistic." She turned away from him
buried her head in her hands. "Gabby, how many times do I have to
tell you? I don't know what I'm doing. I can't promise you I'm not
going to screw up, that I'm not going to hurt you. I can tell you the
sheer thought of hurting you hurts me. I want to try. I am trying.
Will you please try with me?" He mirrored her position.

Gabby sobbed into her hands. She couldn't hold back her emotions
any longer. She was tired from the large meal they had eaten and
her day on the beach. In fact, this day just felt like it was never going to end to her and for the last several hours she had prayed it
wouldn't. But, yet again, she had opened her mouth and ruined
everything.

"Gabby, please," he pleaded. "What's your plan, Bradley? What is
your plan to make this work? Tell me. I can't tell you I'll try until I
know. I can't go home tonight and wonder when you'll call me
again and wait and wait and wait. I can't wonder everyday if it will

be another three months before I get to see you. I'd rather have nothing than to have that." Her frustration was audible in her tone.

"I don't know. I don't know what my plans will be. I mean, I am usually free on the weekends. During the week, I'll be working. You'll be in class. We could Skype, email and text during the week. Hmm, that could be fun," he teased.

She nudged him and barely glancing over at him with her eyes narrowed, she couldn't contain her amusement at his insinuation. Her smile quickly faded because she was trying to be serious and he was bringing up innuendos that took her mind to a place where thinking wasn't welcome.

"Stop it. You're getting way ahead of yourself. And the weekends?" she asked seriously, but with a warm interested smile.

"Well, we could take turns. You know, me come here one weekend, you go to Atlanta the next. Maybe meet halfway?" It was as if he was thinking out loud.

"That's a lot of driving."

"Yeah, I know. I don't know, Gabby. Maybe you're right. I just don't think I can leave you tonight and think that this is over. I don't think I can leave you tonight and even contemplate another man putting his hands on you." He closed his eyes and his mouth formed a firm line as if he was trying to hold back anger. Gabby realized the thought of him with someone else was just as unsettling to her.

"If I agree to this, does that mean we're exclusive," she asked shyly.

"Yes, isn't that what I just said to you?" He looked at her puzzled and almost annoyed.

"No, you said you couldn't think of me with another man. You never mentioned what your intentions were. Obviously, you have needs that I'm not going to be able to meet. I need you to assure me that you won't be with anyone else if we try this."

"Hell, Gabby. No, I haven't been able to be with anyone else since the last time we were right here in this very location. You have my word. What do I have to do to convince you that I wouldn't be going through all this if I wasn't serious?"

"It's just in the past, the word of a man hasn't meant much." She looked back down at the planks of hardwood below her feet. She was nervously bending her knees, moving the swing back and forth. "I am sorry that has been your experience, but I would like a chance to show you that *my* word is good. Please," he begged.

"So, just to be clear. If I say yes, I'll try this crazy long-distance relationship with you that we'll both be exclusive. No other men, no other women. Just us?" She was still unsure. Part of her wanted to hop up and run, to run fast. But, the other part of her was telling her Bradley Banks might just be the one. She owed it to herself to give it a chance. What if she spent the rest of her life waiting for a man she had turned away?

"Yes, Gabriella. You have my word. It will only be you. What do you say?" He was eager, like a boy who was about to get a toy in a toy store.

She looked at him and then she looked out to the water. She could barely think when she was with him and she certainly had trouble thinking when she was looking into his playful blue eyes thinking about how badly she wanted his lips back on hers. She shook her head disapprovingly and closed her eyes and pursed her lips together.

CHAPTER 19

August, 2008

"Gabs, John and I are going to a back-to-school party tomorrow, you wanna come," asked Ian.

"Yep, sounds good. What time?"

"Seven."

"Okay. What are you doing?"

"I'm about to head out to hang out with John and the guys. I gotta go, see you tomorrow?"

"Yes, love you," Gabby quietly muttered.

"Yep, love you, too."

"Bye, Ian."

"See ya."

Ian had been acting so strange the entire summer. Gabby couldn't place her finger on what it was, but he seemed distant.

Gabby had thought Lindsey would call her back later that day in June when John had broken up with her to go on their shopping trip, but she didn't. She had actually never called her back after that. Gabby had tried and tried to talk to Lindsey but no matter what she did, Lindsey refused to see her or speak with her. Gabby had spent the entire summer wondering what she had done to upset Lindsey so badly. She was hurt. She could barely eat, sleep or think of anything but her friend. Gabby had tried to talk to John to see if he knew what Gabby had done to make Lindsey so upset, but Lindsey had also refused to talk to him, as well. After several weeks had gone by, Gabby decided to spend the rest of the summer hanging out with Ian and John. She also spent as much time with Sam as she could, but Sam had taken summer classes again to help get her timing back on track for med school.

Gabby had attended several small parties with their close friends during the summer, but Lindsey was never there. It was as if she knew which parties Gabby would attend and avoided them like she did everything else. She just couldn't understand. Gabby cringed at the thought of being in the same building with Lindsey but not being able to talk to her. She missed her friend. She secretly prayed that Lindsey would come back around and one day give her another chance, or at least tell her what she had done so she would have closure with the relationship. The more Gabby thought about it, it was as if she was in mourning over the loss of their friendship. She felt robbed of the opportunity to try to fix whatever it was she had done in the first place to make Lindsey stop talking to her. She knew that whatever it was must have been really bad because in all the years she had known Lindsey, they had never really had a fight, much less stopped talking to each other. The thought really gnawed at Gabby because she couldn't even apologize to Lindsey. She wouldn't know what she was even apologizing for.

The horn honked and Gabby jumped up and grabbed her purse, cell phone and keys as she ran to the door. She grinned as she ran down the sidewalk to Ian's car.

"Hey you," she cheerfully greeted him. "Hey, yourself," he smiled back at her. "Are you okay?" Gabby was concerned with his shortness. "Yes, why wouldn't I be?"

"You just have been different lately."

"No, I haven't. Maybe it's you who's different."

Gabby couldn't help but feel hurt by his tone and the insinuation that she was the one who had changed. She sat in the seat feeling like a child and reflecting on her own behavior. *Had she been the one to change? Was that what was wrong with Lindsey?* No, she was the same as she had always been. Maybe they were all just growing apart.

"Ian?"

"What?"

"If we weren't okay, would you tell me," she glanced over at him as she twirled her fingers together in her lap.

"Yeah, I guess. I mean, what's wrong with you today. Why are you asking me about all of this? Are you trying to tell me something?" He never looked at her and his expression was impassive.

"No! I'm not trying to tell you something. I'm trying to find out why you've been so cold. You used to be so affectionate with me.

We hardly do anything anymore. You're short and confrontational about everything. I just don't understand. Have I done something wrong? Is it because I won't have sex with you?"

"Gabby, please. Are we seriously about to have this conversation again? How many times do we have to rehash this," he was irritated.

"You didn't answer me, Ian," she said quietly. "Gabby, we've had this conversation before. My answer hasn't changed. I wish you'd just leave it alone already. I told you I wanted to be with you. We're fine. Now, can we just enjoy the night?"

"Yes, I'm sorry." She put her head down upset that she had already managed to ruin the night.

When they arrived to the party, everyone was already there. They made their casual slightly late appearance and all of Ian's friends whisked him away. "Hey Gabs, make yourself at home. I'll be right back," he walked away letting go of her hand.

This was not quite the way she had pictured the party going, but she understood he had not seen his friends much during the summer. But, then again, he had not seen her much during the summer, either. She couldn't help but feel like she was at the very bottom of his priority list. She felt their connection slipping through her fingertips and there was nothing she seemed to be able to do to make it stop. She got herself a diet coke and plopped down on the couch and smiled as she watched teenagers doing silly dances making fools out of themselves. She vowed to dismiss her thoughts for the night and just enjoy the party and the beginning of what would be her last year of high school.

CHAPTER 20

August, 2010; *The Present*

"Is that a no," Bradley asked his voice quiet and sad.

Gabby looked up into his broken blue eyes and continued to shake her head. The thought of breaking his heart would break hers. She wanted to run away from *this* so badly like she had done at the reception. But, she had a feeling if she ran this time there would be no other chances. She could hear the hurt in his voice and she was pretty sure that if she said no, Bradley would accept it and he would never pursue her again. This was his last ditch effort and he was already out of his comfort zone. She feared her rejection would only make him reject commitment that much more in the future. The thought of being the reason for his brokenness was too much for her to bear. She had been on the bearing front of that kind of hurt before and she knew just how unbearable it was. She chewed on her bottom lip and she grabbed all of her hair pushing it behind her shoulders. She suddenly felt like she couldn't breathe in the dress that he had picked out for her earlier in the evening and she was lightheaded.

"Gabby, are you okay," he asked growing concerned. "Why won't you talk to me? What are you thinking? It's okay. Just say something so I'll know you're okay," he urged her.

"I am so scared."

"I know. Maybe I should give you some time to think it over. I shouldn't have put you on the spot. Ever since I showed up today, that's all I've done, put you on the spot. I'm sorry. I'm not used to this, any of this. I'm used to getting my way and pretty quickly. I'm like a spoiled little boy who only has to ask once and he gets exactly what he wants and then some. But, you're different. It is just going to take some time for me to get used to this." He shrugged his shoulders and his eyes never left hers.

"But, don't you get it. You shouldn't have to change who you are to be with someone. You should be able to be yourself, one hundred percent. If you've already had to change to be around me, *this* isn't really right," she pleaded.

"Gabby, I needed to change who I was. It's a change for the better, I assure you. And, if I didn't want to change, I wouldn't be here. You can't make someone change unless they want to change. I learned this the hard way growing up, but you make me want to change. You make me want to be a better man and I only just met you. I can only imagine the man I will become if you will give me a chance, Gabby."

"Oh, I doubt that. I don't know how I can make anyone better. I am messed up. There's stuff in my past that I have never dealt with and I'm not sure I can deal with it. I'm not sure I can be what you need me to be." She put her head back down as she felt tears springing into her eyes again as she reflected on her conversation with Sam earlier about therapy.

"But, that's it. You are. You are what I need. It took me the last two and a half months to figure that out, but I know now and I'm not going to let you tell me what I do and don't need." He said sternly but softly. He stroked the side of her cheek and pushed the stray piece of hair that had fallen from her shoulders behind her right ear.

"When are you leaving?" she asked.

"Sunday."

"Can I have some time to think about it then?" She looked back into his eyes. She knew she didn't stand a chance at resisting him, but maybe he would think about their night and change his mind and she wouldn't have to answer him at all.

"Can I see you again while I'm here?" he playfully smiled.

"Are you saying I can only think about it if I agree to see you again?" Her eyes were growing larger at the thought of the game she knew he had just started.

"I would like to hear your answer in person. I'd really like to spend every moment of my time here with you, but I respect that you didn't come home to see me. You came to see your sister."

"You're right about that, Mr. Banks," she smirked.

"Hmm." He closed his eyes as he smiled.

"So, Miss Gerhart, am I going to see you again?"

"I suppose if you want your answer in person then we should meet tomorrow night. This time I get to pick where we eat and what I have to wear." She grinned.

"Deal. Shall I take you home then, or would you like to just spend a little more time swinging?" His tone had other implications than swinging.

"Um, I think it might be best for me to get home so I can think about your proposition. I have trouble thinking when I'm near you. And. I don't think swinging is what you have in mind, anyway, Mr. Banks." She nudged him flirtatiously.

"You have me all figured out, it takes every ounce of control in my being to keep my hands off you when I'm around you. I most definitely want to kiss you again, but I am a gentleman, or at least trying to be, so I will take you home." He stood and held his hand out to her to help her off the swing.

"Thank you, Bradley. I mean, until I ruined our moment, this had been one of the best nights of my life. I know you went through a lot of trouble. Thank you." She smiled up into his sparkling blue eyes.

"Then say yes." He reached down and planted a soft kiss on her lips.

"It's not that simple and you know it." Her eyes still closed from his kiss.

"Anything worth having is never simple or easy, Gabby."

"You may be right, but I'm not sure. You told me I could think about it."

"I know, I am just anxious. I'm never going to be able to make it until tomorrow night. It's going to be torture. Now that I've seen you again and I've felt this, I don't want for it to end. Part of me wants to take you into that beautiful building right there and carry you to my room and just hold you and watch you sleep for the rest of the night. You make me greedy for you. I just can't get enough. I can see the way your body reacts to me. I know the feeling is mutual. I wish you would just accept it for what it is and trust me," he confessed.

Gabby was finding it harder and harder to control herself. He was right, every ounce of her body reacted to his every move, to his proximity. Her body wanted for her to kiss him for hours and the thought of sleeping in the bed with him being held in his strong arms brought an unusual feeling of comfort. But, she knew her body wasn't always to be trusted. She just had to think about it outside of his presence. She knew she couldn't talk to Sam about it because she already knew how Sam felt about him. If anything, Sam was on Bradley's side. At times like this she really missed the friendship she once had with Lindsey, but that had been over since the summer before senior year and then she remembered, was Lindsey ever really a friend. She certainly wasn't worthy of being missed.

"Gabby. Let's go. Let me get you home." Bradley interrupted her thoughts and she smiled a polite smile, "Okay."

Bradley quickly got out of the car and hopped over to Gabby's side to open the door for her holding his hand out to help her out of the seat. He reached into the back seat and pulled out her bag of clothes she had been wearing when he met her earlier that night, "Here, don't forget these," he reminded her.

"Ah, thank you. Although, I *will* see you tomorrow night. You could have brought them to me, if I had forgotten them," she winked.

"Oh, I am looking forward to tomorrow night. But me keeping your clothes wouldn't have been a good thing. I would have been very tempted to sleep with them," he chuckled.

Gabby blushed as her jaw dropped. "Mr. Banks, you are quite the...um... I don't know, words fail me." She giggled.

"You have no idea." He proudly grinned stroking the side of her cheek.

"Gabby, thank you for tonight. Please promise me you'll think about this and make your decision not out of fear," he urged her.

She closed her eyes savoring his touch, "I promise."

"Open your eyes, Gabby. Look at me," he commanded.

She immediately blinked her eyes open and stared into his deter-mined blue eyes, how she would miss those eyes if she said no.

"Look me in the eyes and promise me that you will not make your decision out of fear, Gabby. I'm a really good judge of character and I can tell if you're lying to me. I want you to look me in the eyes and promise me that." He was very serious.

Gabby looked into his eyes, then she looked away. She knew deep down that the reason she had not made eye contact with him was because she had intended to turn him down and she knew deep down that it was because of fear. How was he able to do this to her, to break down walls with her so quickly. She was able to communi-cate things with him that in other situations would have made her too scared to say.

"Look at me, say it."

She looked back into his blazing eyes, "I promise." She smiled.

She was surprised at how good it felt to promise him and really mean it and to promise herself that she would really consider this and try to put fear aside. She was suddenly sad to see him leave her. She stretched her arms around his neck and ran her fingers through the back of his hair at the nape of his neck.

"Bradley, what have you done to me," she smiled up at him with an awestruck look.

He wrapped his arms around her waist and pulled her close and the shift took her breath away. "The feeling is mutual, Miss Gerhart. I have no idea what you have done to me, but I must say, I like it. I don't want it to end." He smiled as he rubbed his nose against hers.

"Me neither," she had said it before her mind could filter it and the words were out, there was no turning back now. His eyes lit up and he immediately pulled her as close as he could and his mouth took hers in a passionate kiss filled with relief, hope, and anticipation of what the future might hold for them.

CHAPTER 21

August, 2008

Ian had gone upstairs to use the bathroom and clear his head. He knew Gabby knew something was not right and he was so torn. Things had changed, but he didn't know how to tell her just how much things had changed. He knew that if he were to tell her what was really going on she would not only be heartbroken, but furious.

As he exited the bathroom with his head down, he was running his fingers through his long locks, when he ran into her.

"Linds, what in the hell are you doing here? You know you can't be here. She's downstairs," Ian growled with his teeth clenched. He grabbed her elbow and pulled her into a bedroom.

Lindsey answered not with words but with a long passionate kiss and pushed him up against the door. It took everything in Ian to push her away.

"Linds, we can't. Not here. Stop," he pleaded but not pushing her away.

"I don't care that she's here. I'm sick of hiding. Why won't you just break up with her already," Lindsey spoke breathlessly through her kiss.

"It will totally break her, you know that. This is wrong, but I just can't help myself. You. Are. Irresistible." He said each word a staccato and he pushed her onto the bed.

Lindsey giggled and Ian put his finger over her mouth, "Shh, if we're going to do this here, you've got to be quiet," he commanded.

"Okay, do you have condoms," she asked.

"Yes, always prepared. Although I must admit this was a pleasant surprise. Now, no more talking, we don't have a lot of time." He smiled a smug grin.

Ian climbed over Lindsey on the bed and started to nibble her ear lobe. He knew how much she liked that and she wiggled underneath him. "Be still," he softly said as he moved to her jaw line and then to her mouth. Lindsey had worn a skirt making access easy for him, and so he pushed the skirt up around her waist and he moved her lace panties to the side and slid in a finger. "Ah, you're so ready." Lindsey smiled, "I'm always ready for you, Ian." He removed her panties and threw them to the side of the bed. He opened his wallet and removed his condom and unbuttoned his shorts. He slid the condom over his erection and sank himself into her releasing a moan. Lindsey wrapped her arms around his waist, her mouth forming an O and she gasped for air.

Gabby glanced down at her speedo watch and realized that Ian had been gone for nearly an hour. She had spent that time thinking back to the party they had gone to almost a year ago at John's, the first party they went to together as a couple. Ian had been so wonderful to her. He had a large bouquet of flowers for her when he met her at the door. Emma had immediately found Ian charming and he talked at ease with her, acting far more mature than most boys she knew their age. He waited for Gabby to finish getting ready knowing already that she was always late. He had opened the doors for her, held her hand, and made her feel like she was the most adored girl. She was sure that by that night she had already fallen in love with him. She adored Ian and was so excited when she arrived to the party and had seen that Lindsey and John had finally hit it off and were getting cozy with one another. Within a couple of weeks, Lindsey and John were a couple and the four of them went out every weekend. Thinking about this confirmed for Gabby what she had tried to deny for the entire summer. Any doubts she had that things were all in her head about the changes she felt in their relationship were now gone. She knew something was not right with Ian and she would not believe for another minute it was her. She was the same as she had always been. She adored Ian and would do anything for him, including going to parties she really didn't like, just to be with him. He never left her side at those parties, knowing she was only there for him. But, tonight, he had not just left her, he had been gone for far too long. Gabby got up determined to find him and ask him to take her home. She was tired and this was not fun at all. She needed some time to think about what to do. She knew she wanted to work it out and she wanted answers for why he had changed. She just wasn't sure how to even begin the conversation. Every time she had tried during the summer, Ian had always brushed her off. She would not back down or be pushed to believe this was her fault any longer. She was confused because she wasn't sure why he had even asked her to come if he had no intention of being with her. Was he just stringing her along?

Gabby made her way to the kitchen and the group of guys Ian had been hanging out with when they arrived were all gathered around the bar.

"Hey, I thought Ian was with you. Have you seen him," Gabby inquired.

"No, Gabby. He left us about twenty minutes or so ago. We thought he went to find you."

"Hmm, obviously not. If you see him will you tell him I'm looking for him."

"Yeah, sure."

Gabby walked around the downstairs and randomly asked people if they had seen Ian. Finally someone said they had seen him head upstairs by himself. She found this unnerving. Why would he come to a party to be alone, unless he wasn't? Her stomach cramped and her gut told her not to go upstairs, but her curiosity got the best of her. She had to know what was going on with him and more than anything she just wanted to go home.

Gabby held the railing of the stairs as she climbed taking a deep breath with each step and exhaling the excess air. When she reached the top and saw the hall was clear, she began slowly opening each door. When she reached the last door, she heard a noise. When she opened it, she could not believe her eyes. In that moment, her heart fell out of her chest and like a glass vase filled with the flowers he had brought her, dropped onto a concrete floor and shattered into a million small pieces. She was sure there would be no way to ever be put it back together.

CHAPTER 22

August, 2010; The Present

"Oh, Gabby," Bradley spoke softly and relieved, he leaned down and lifted her chin with his forefinger and thumb and he kissed her passionately as if his life depended on her touch. Their tongues twisted and turned and she used her fingers to tug on his hair and hold his head tightly.

She pulled away, "I didn't mean to say that," she closed her eyes and put her head down.

"I know you didn't mean to say it, but you said it because you feel it. You had a moment where you didn't let fear dictate your words and even though I know you want this, it was nice to hear it."

"I do want it, Bradley. I just don't see how in the world it is ever going to work."

"It's certainly never going to work if we don't try." He smiled.

"I know."

"Gabby, I'm not ready for this night to end. Do you want to go change into these clothes and go for a walk on the beach? We could talk some more." He gestured holding her clothes up in front of her face and cocked his head to one side. His eyes were filled with eager anticipation.

"Okay."

Gabby and Bradley walked to the beach from her house. When they got to the sand, they removed their shoes and Bradley rolled up the bottoms of his pristine trousers. He took both sets of their shoes into his large hands and he had the bag they had prepared at Gabby's with a blanket for them to sit on hanging from his shoulder. He placed his free hand in hers.

"I love the beach at night," Gabby sighed as she smiled and looked over and up into his eyes.

"Me too," he smiled back.

"Well, actually, I don't think there is a time I don't love the beach, but I really like it at night. There's just something so calming about it at night," she rambled.

"I would have to agree, Miss Gerhart. Shall we find a place to sit or do you want to keep walking?"

"No, I think I'd like to sit. Those shoes you bought me gave me quite the workout earlier," she winked.

"Well, you looked lovely. You should always wear heels like those. You have beautiful legs, Gabby. You're beautiful."

Gabby blushed and smiled as she looked down.

"Let's sit here. The tide won't come back in for a little bit." Gabby pointed to the spot in the soft sand where she wanted to sit.

Bradley spread the blanket out and put their shoes on each corner to hold it down. They both plopped down and leaned back against their palms.

"Gabby, what was his name?" he asked.

"Whose name?"

"The jerk."

"Oh. Ian."

"What did he do to you?"

Gabby shook her head and looked down.

"Please tell me. I don't want to hurt you. I need to know why you are this broken. I want to know what the asshole did to you."

"I'd had a crush on him for four years. We were at a party, he came onto me. We made out, but he said when we were done he wasn't ready for a relationship. We just kinda kept our relationship a secret for a month or so. Then, he asked me to be his girlfriend. We dated for about a year. We were really serious. That February, he had set up a really special night for us to take it further. I turned him down. I just had him on this pedestal and refused to see that he was such a jerk. Things were never the same after that night. My best friend, Lindsey, had been dating his best friend, John. John and I are like brother and sister. That's a different story, but John broke up with her. She apparently thought John and I were doing something on the sly, but we weren't. Lindsey just quit talking to me. She never told me why. It was like one day she was my best friend and the next she was dead. She refused to talk to me, take my calls, and see me. I had no idea what I had done to her.

In August, Ian asked me to go to this party. I hated parties in high school, but there wasn't much I wouldn't do for him. Well, in fact, there was only one thing I wouldn't do for him. He left me at the party for a bit to be with his friends. Eventually, I went to find him. When I did, he was with Lindsey. I didn't even know Lindsey was at the party. She had avoided us the entire summer, or so I thought. Apparently, she was avoiding me, but not my boyfriend. She gave him exactly what I refused to give him," she shrugged her shoulders and put her head back down as a tear streamed down her face.

She could see in his profile from the light of the moon that his jaw was clenched and his teeth were grinding, his anger was palpable. His eyes were narrowed and were blazing into the ocean. He had sat up during her confession and he was hugging his knees and twisting his fists together.

"Say something. I've never talked about this with anyone other than Sam," Gabby pleaded.

"I hope I never see the little prick's face," he hissed.

"Well, that makes two of us." Gabby let out a slight laugh.

"I'm serious, Gabby." He looked over at her and his expression softened.

"No wonder you're scared to death and think you can't meet my needs. The only man, no boy, you've ever been with was a total dick to you because you wouldn't sleep with him. As if that wasn't enough, he slept with your best friend and you had to witness their tryst. Sick S.O.B."

"Yep, pretty much. And I am sorry, but your timing sucks. August is a month I loathe."

"Yeah, I'm sorry. I'm not like him, Gabby. I promise. I won't be him."

"Part of me believes you. The other part of me never thought Ian or Lindsey would do that to me. If those two people could do that to me, what's stopping you?"

"Let me show you. You don't know me well enough for me to have earned your trust, but all I can do is promise and try every day to show you that I am not that little boy and as for Lindsey, if she did that to you, she was never really your friend."

"I know that now. I had just gotten over that when I saw you at the wedding. My senior year was an absolute nightmare. The only friend I felt like I had was John, who lost his best friend in Ian. He was so pissed at what Ian and Lindsey had done. He could hardly look at Ian again. We spent our senior year watching them hang all over each other. It was disgusting. I couldn't wait for the year to end. I basically went to school and that was it. I didn't go to parties, or anything. I just tried to survive. When I moved in with Sam for college, she took me to some parties and I was so relieved to be around people whom I didn't know and the alcohol I had never been a fan of took the edge off all the raw emotions. I was really in a dark place. It took all year to get me to finally open up again and come out of my shell. Then there was you." Her confession was a relief and it had come so easily.

"Yeah, I can see why you ran away from me. I honestly wouldn't blame you for running again, but really Gabby, I care so much for you already and I don't know what is going to happen with this, but I think we both owe it to each other to give it a try." He leaned over and cupped her face with his hand.

"I'm still so broken. There are other things you don't know about me. There are things I don't even remember that I have suppressed somewhere deep inside of me, things from my past. I just don't know if I can do anything until I figure that stuff out and put it behind me, not buried deep inside of me."

"Gabby, we all have a past. I get that. Maybe we should just slow down and get to know each other. If things are meant to be, I suppose they will be. I just find it very difficult to not touch you. But, there is the distance factor and maybe that would help if we weren't in a serious relationship. If we were just friends at first, would that make you feel better?"

"I don't know. I definitely feel this and it is hard not to explore it. Your touch, your proximity, as much as they scare me also make me feel safe and I haven't felt that way in a long time. I do think this is moving too fast for me, though. We don't even know each other. And, then there's the whole distance thing. I'm not sure that's something I can deal with. But, maybe if we're just friends at first, we'll be able to acclimate to that and it will make it more natural if it moves forward. Is it possible to go back though? Is it possible to forget that we've kissed and what it felt like?"

"I don't know. I know I can't forget it. I tried for months to forget it and here I am. I'm not going to lie, I have ulterior motives. I want this to go further, but I am willing to wait and give you some time. I want it to work, more than I've ever wanted anything. I don't want to screw it up because I'm too impatient. I've already done that once and I will utilize all of my self-control to try to avoid that again."

"You had said if we did this that you would be exclusive, but obviously if we're just friends, there's no way you will be happy. You'll resent me. I've been there done that, remember?"

"He was an ass. He was stupid to not realize what he had. He didn't and doesn't deserve you. I don't want to be compared to him. I am not him. I will work it out somehow. I am willing to try. If it's not working out, I promise to talk to you about it. I won't do anything until we've talked. Is that fair?"

"Bradley, you know well enough that when you are in a situation, you aren't going to have the frame of mind to think *hmm, I need to talk to the girl who's not my girlfriend before I do anything.* I appreciate your idea, but it's not practical." She let out a sarcastic laugh and shook her head disapprovingly.

"I honestly can't see me putting myself in that situation. I haven't for the past two months and there was no commitment, Gabby. If I give you my word, you will have my word. I understand that my word means very little to you, as I've done nothing to earn your trust. But, I'm here. I'm trying. Please, just tell me what I have to do. I'll take whatever I can get. If it's friendship, I'll take it. I just can't leave and never see you or talk to you again. That is not enough," he closed his eyes and pursed his lips.

"I guess no one really has trust in the beginning, huh?" she pondered her words and his.

"No, I think in every relationship trust is built. I think when you've had someone break your trust, it is harder to trust again, but you can't assume that everyone is like him. Not everyone is a slime ball."

"So, we'd just be friends. Exclusive friends?" She couldn't help but bust out laughing at the ridiculousness of the phrase. She realized it was the opposite of what she and Ian had started as. He was asking her to start her second relationship the way it should be, with the foundation being a non-physical relationship, the building of a friendship and if there was more, then eventually building that, as well.

"Gabby, I promise. I will wait for you. But, you have to promise to talk to me. I want to see you. We'll work out the weekends. We'll take trips and go to dinner. We'll go shopping. We'll do normal fun stuff that you have lost out on because of the jerk. You'll get some help for these other issues and when it's time, we'll move it forward."

"Sam has already said that she would find someone through school to help us."

"Help you both? Gabby, what in the hell happened to the two of you?"

"I don't know. Sam remembers. I know it was bad. I just have put it out of my mind for so long. I was only five. It was something with my dad, but I don't know. The only thing I know is that my mom left him because of me."

"Oh, Gabby." He reached over and put his arms around her shoulders and pulled her in. "I don't want you getting help from anyone who isn't the best in their profession. You aren't going to be some guinea pig for a med student or resident. I'll find the very best in the area and I'll arrange for sessions for both you and Sam."

"I can't let you do that. That's too much." She looked up into his eyes, but she could see the resolve and she knew it wasn't up for discussion.

"It's done, it's not up for conversation or debate. I'll let you know who I find on Monday. Am I understood?" His voice was kind but stern, with a sweet protective undertone.

"Yes. Thank you." She put her head down and fidgeted with her fingers.

"We should go, it's really late. I don't want you to be so tired you can't enjoy your time with Sam," he said as he looked out to the horizon.

"I am excited about *this*. Thank you for tonight, Bradley. I can't begin to tell you how lovely it has been."

"I'm excited, too. And, no, thank you, Gabby." He took her fingers and gently pulled her hand to his lips and placed a long sweet kiss on the top of her knuckles.

The pair picked up the blanket and shook it to get the sand off and they packed it back into their bag. Bradley took their shoes into one hand and threw the bag over his shoulder. He walked with his hand protectively around the lower part of her back the entire way home. As they approached the driveway, he stopped and faced her.

"Can I still see you tomorrow evening? Are we still going to dinner?" he was stroking her hair as he spoke the words in almost a whisper. The charge between the two of them was so strong, but he knew he had to try not to be too affectionate. He didn't want her to get scared, second guess her decision and change her mind about trying.

"Yes, I'd like that."

"Good. I'll pick you up at seven. What should I wear?" He couldn't help but grin at their earlier conversation that she would be picking attire and food.

"Casual, comfortable, and seven sounds great."

He could see her eyes were tired and she could barely keep them open.

"Let me walk you to your door, make sure you get inside okay."

"Thank you, Bradley."

"For what?"

She shrugged her shoulders and looked at the ground. Then her eyes were blazing as she looked back up at him.

"For everything. For finding me and not letting me run away this time. For being a gentleman. Goodnight."

His eyes sparkled off the front porch light that Sam had left on for Gabby and he smiled releasing a sigh as he pushed her hair back behind her ears.

"Anything for you, Gabby. Good night, I'll see you later, it's already tomorrow."

Gabby giggled and Bradley leaned in and placed a sweet kiss on her forehead and released her and walked to his car.

He opened the door and grinned to himself like a school boy. He would make sure he found the best therapist for her and Sam Charleston had to offer on Monday. He would spend all of his free time making sure he could be near her, no matter the cost, and his newest mission was to win her, to worship her, to love her.

Visit **www.jbmcgee.com** to stay up to date on news regarding the release of the second book in the *This* series, *Mending*.

About the Author

J.B. McGee was born and raised in Aiken, South Carolina. After graduating from South Aiken High School, she toured Europe as a member of the 1999 International Bands of America Tour, playing the clarinet. While attending Converse College, an all-girls school in Spartanburg, South Carolina, she visited Charleston often. It quickly became one of her favorite vacation spots. She met her husband, Chad, during Christmas break of her freshman year, and they married in 2001 and she moved back to her hometown. In 2005, the couple welcomed their first son, Noah. J.B. finished her Bachelor of Arts degree in Early Childhood Education at the University of South Carolina-Aiken in 2006. During her time studying children's literature, a professor had encouraged her to become a writer.

In 2007, she welcomed their second child, Jonah, and she became a stay at home mom/entrepreneur. In 2009, they found out their two children and J.B. have Mitochondrial Disease. In 2011, a diagnosis also was given to Chad. Please take a moment and learn more about Mitochondrial Disease. Awareness is key to this disease that has no cure or treatments. *www.foundmm.org*

J.B. McGee and her family now reside in Buford, Georgia, to be closer to their children's medical team. After a passion for reading had been re-ignited, J.B. decided to finally give writing a shot. *Broken* (*This* Series), is her first book and first series.

ACKNOWLEDGMENTS

To my mom and dad, Taylor Swift says it best. "Standing back and watching me shine, and I didn't know if you knew but I am taking this chance to say that I had the best day with you, today." You have always stood back and watched me shine. Whether it was dance, cheering, sports, band, monogramming, web design, or writing a book, your support has been unwavering. One of my biggest goals in life has been to make you proud.

Amanda, my big sister, my Sam. I am so thankful that we both got to go through the process of publishing our first books at the same time, sharing all these crazy emotions that come with it. I cherish every moment I get to spend being your sister.

Emily, Debi, Dee Dee, Joanne, Trish, Gwendolyn, Lora, and Jessica; you were my very first readers. You were true friends, telling me what was terrible and what was great. Thank you for being so incredibly supportive of this process and cheering me on when I was down, for always encouraging me to keep going.